EDGAR ALLAN POE

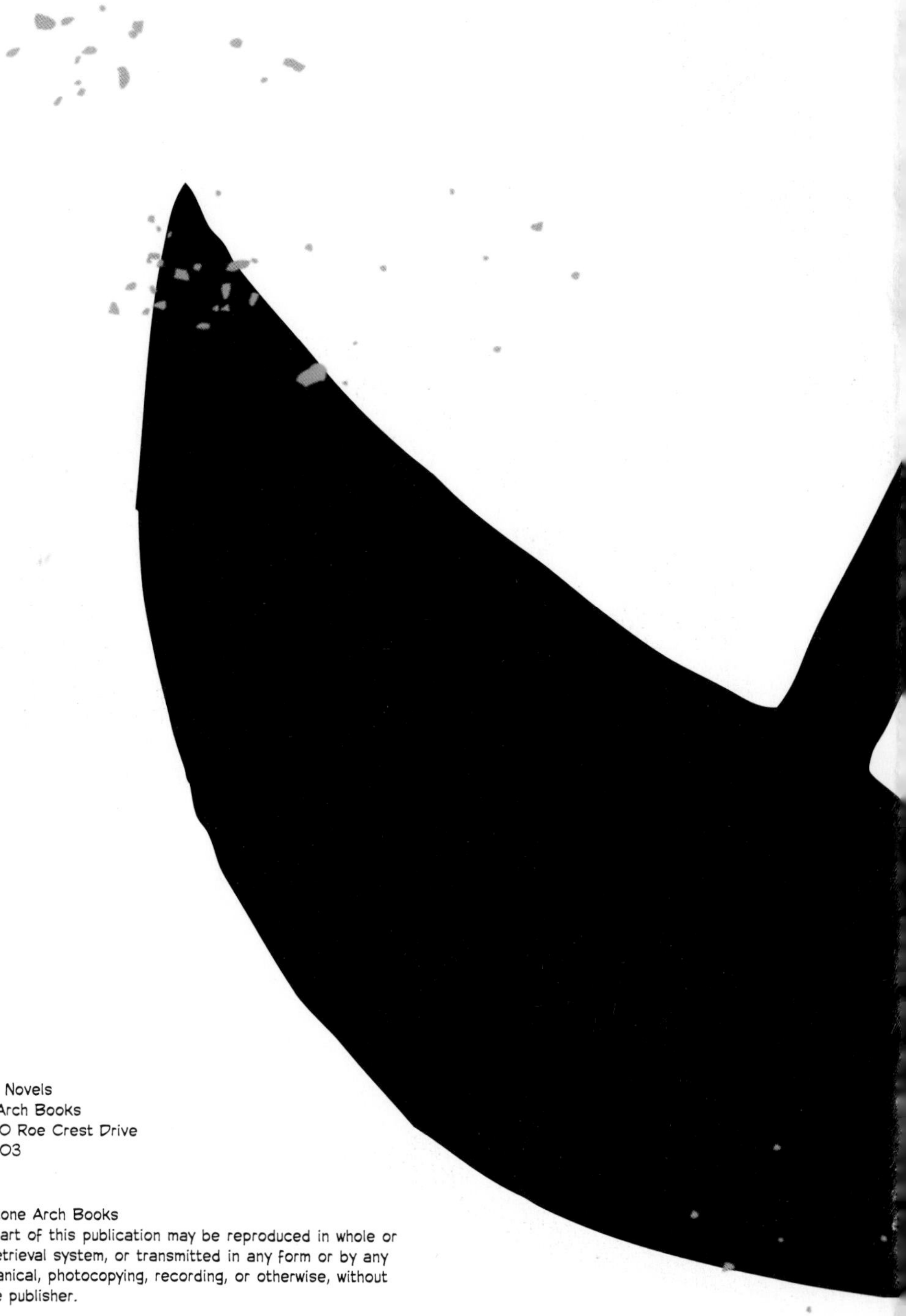

Edgar Allan Poe Graphic Novels
are published by Stone Arch Books
A Capstone Imprint, 1710 Roe Crest Drive
North Mankato, MN 56003
www.capstonepub.com

Cataloging-in-Publication Data is available on the Library of Congress website.

ISBN: 978-1-4342-4024-8 (library binding)
ISBN: 978-1-4342-4260-0 (paperback)
ISBN: 978-1-4342-5967-7 (eBook)

Summary: Sentenced to death by the Inquisition, a desperate man awaits his fate locked in a dark dungeon. There's a bottomless pit below him. A razor sharp pendulum swings from above. Hideous demons are carved into the metal walls. The man's only companions are beady-eyed rats and the echo of his own terrified voice. When the demons start to smile, he begins to wonder if he has lost his mind...

Art Director: Bob Lentz
Graphic Designers: Hilary Wacholz and Brann Garvey
Edited by: Donald Lemke

Printed in the United States of America in North Mankato, Minnesota.
042013 007308R

THE PIT AND THE PENDULUM

BY EDGAR ALLAN POE

RETOLD BY SEAN TULIEN

ILLUSTRATED BY J.C. FABUL

STONE ARCH BOOKS · A CAPSTONE IMPRINT

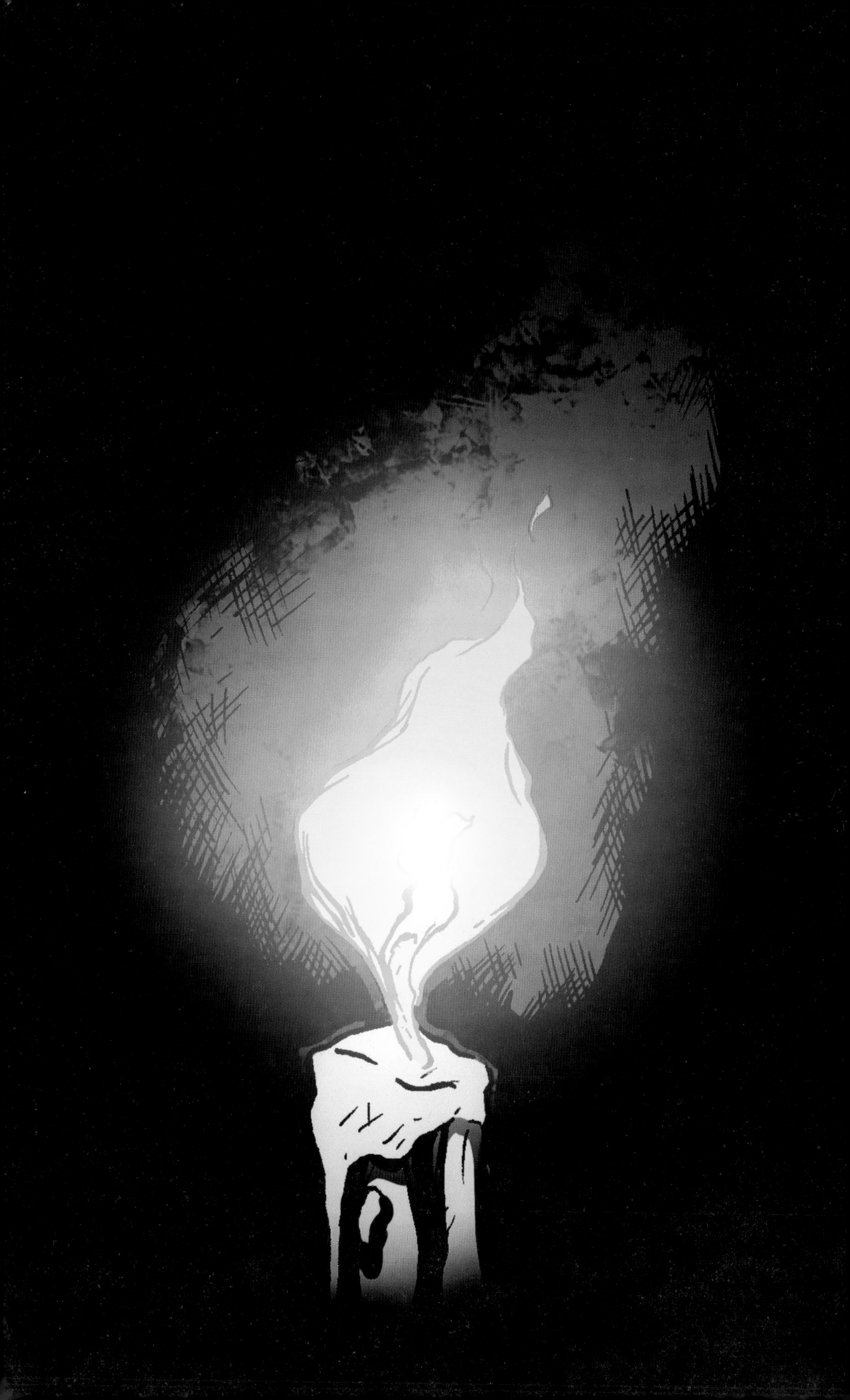

Here a wicked mob of torturers long fed their
undying thirst for innocent blood. Now that the
homeland is saved, and the cave of murder is
destroyed, life and health appear where grim
death once was...

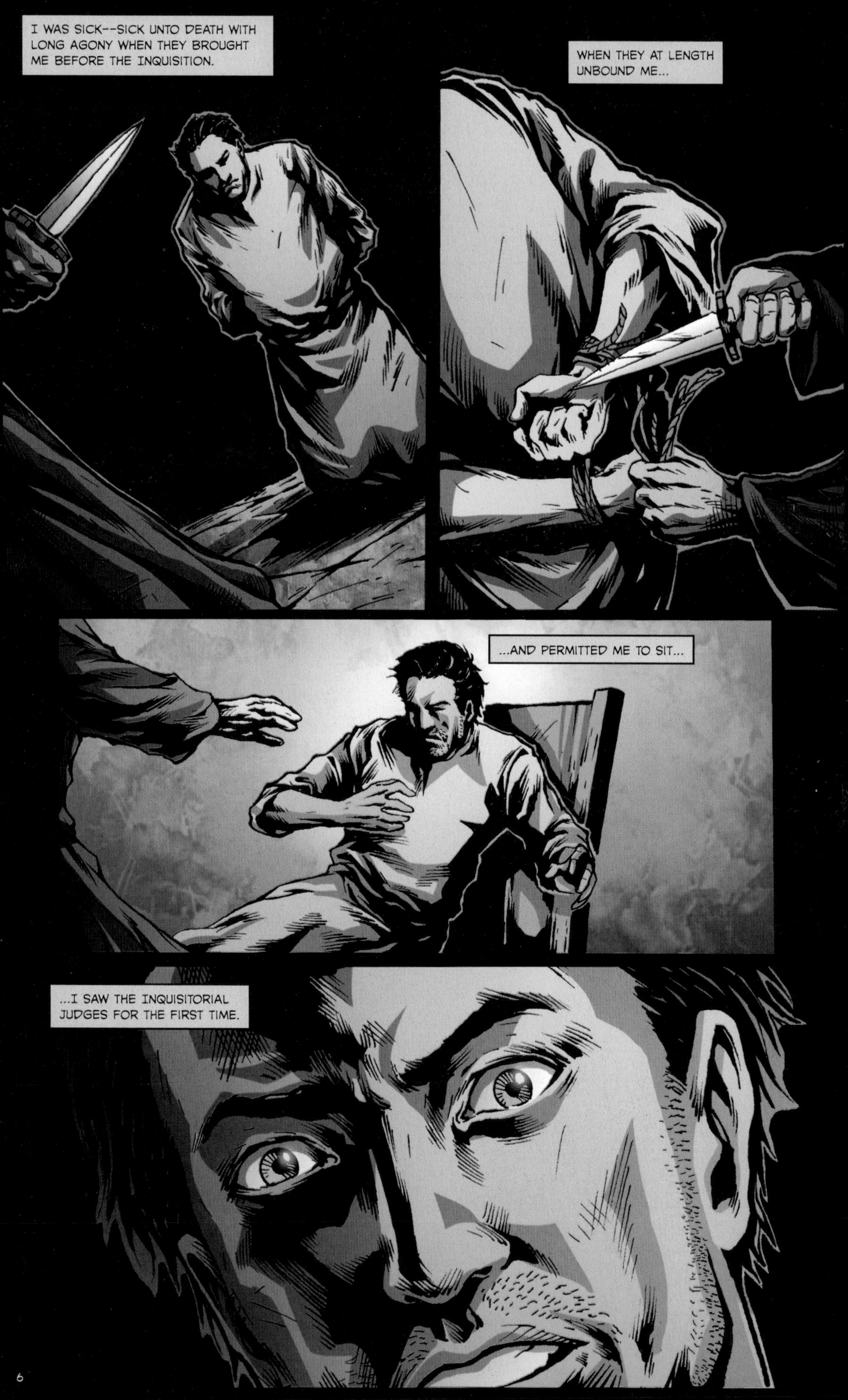
I WAS SICK--SICK UNTO DEATH WITH LONG AGONY WHEN THEY BROUGHT ME BEFORE THE INQUISITION.
WHEN THEY AT LENGTH UNBOUND ME...
...AND PERMITTED ME TO SIT...
...I SAW THE INQUISITORIAL JUDGES FOR THE FIRST TIME.

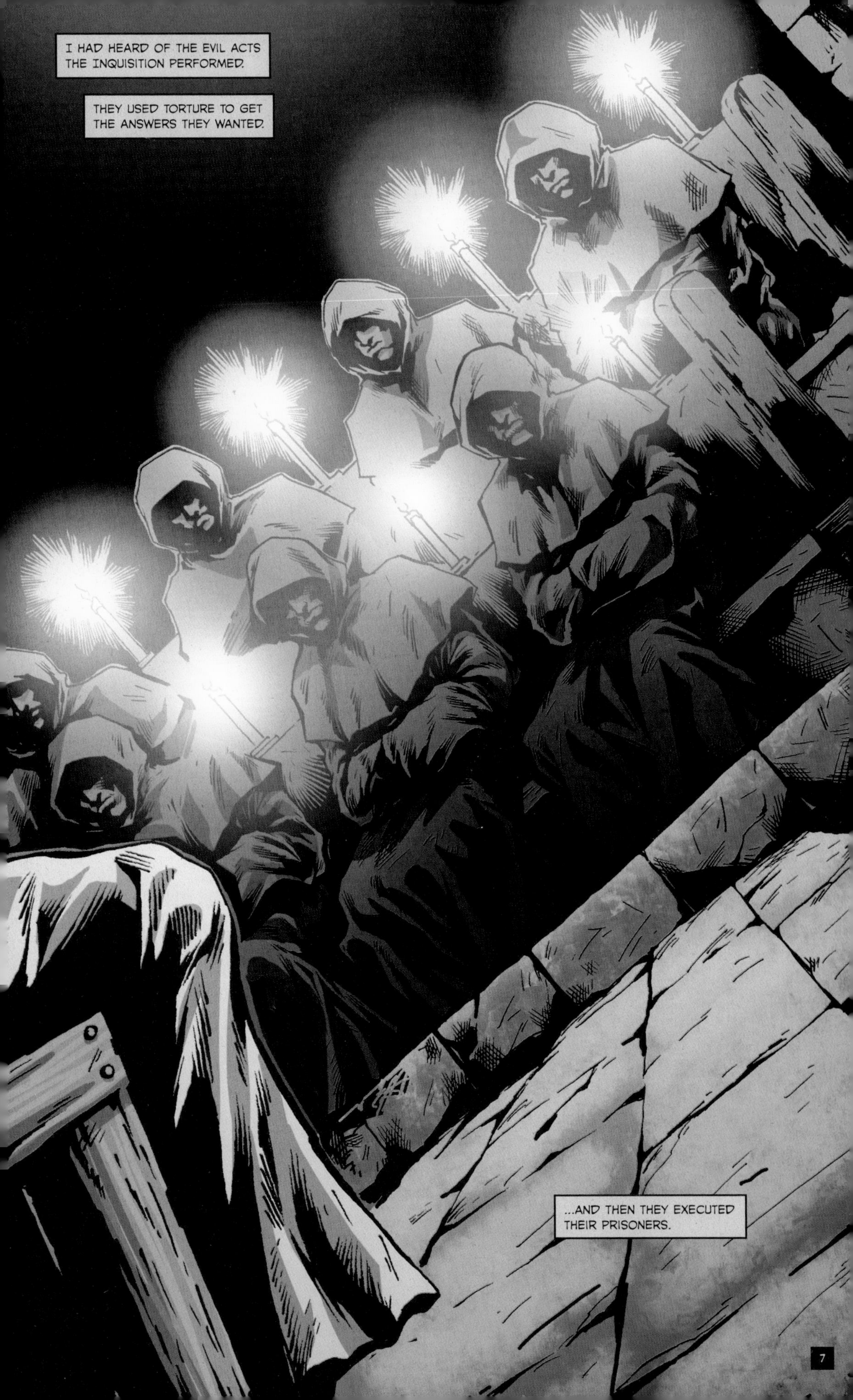
I HAD HEARD OF THE EVIL ACTS THE INQUISITION PERFORMED.
THEY USED TORTURE TO GET THE ANSWERS THEY WANTED.
...AND THEN THEY EXECUTED THEIR PRISONERS.

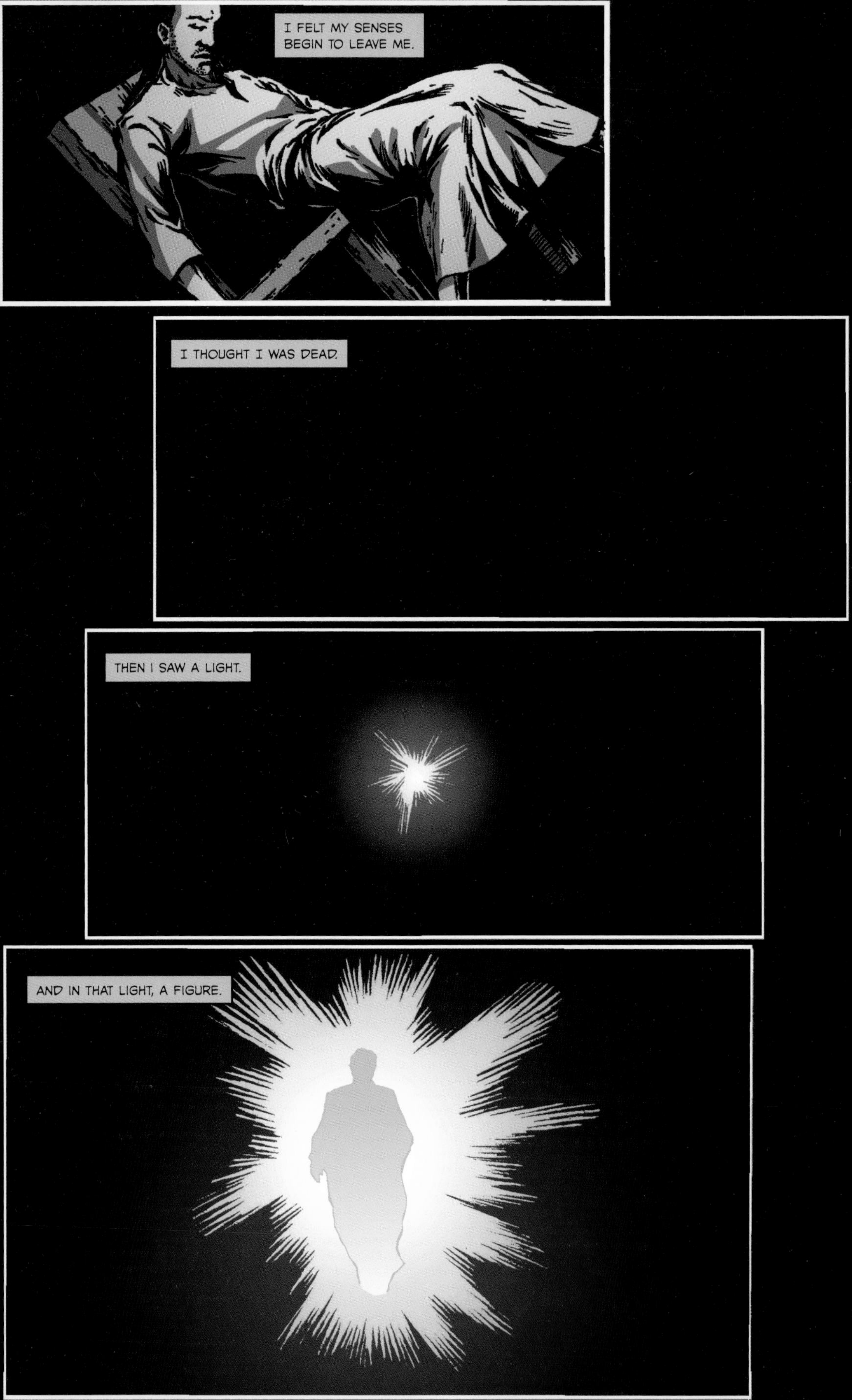
I FELT MY SENSES BEGIN TO LEAVE ME.
I THOUGHT I WAS DEAD.
THEN I SAW A LIGHT.
AND IN THAT LIGHT, A FIGURE.

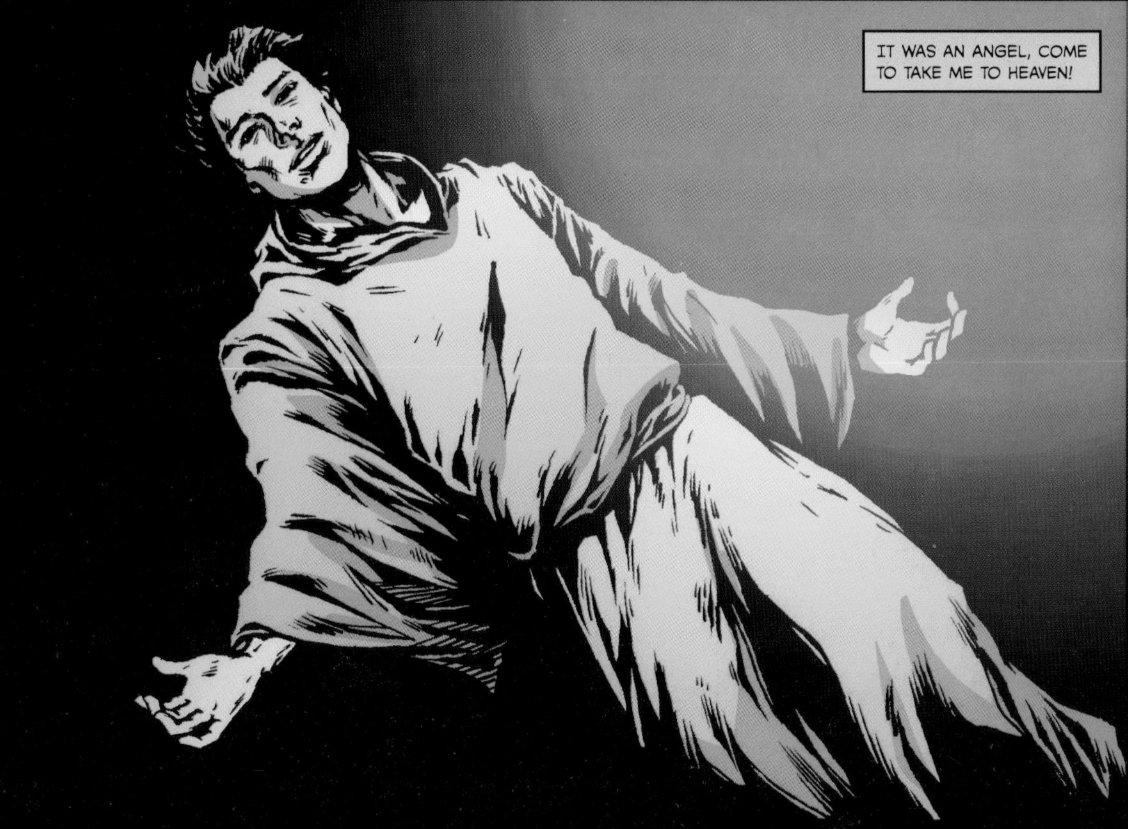
IT WAS AN ANGEL, COME TO TAKE ME TO HEAVEN!

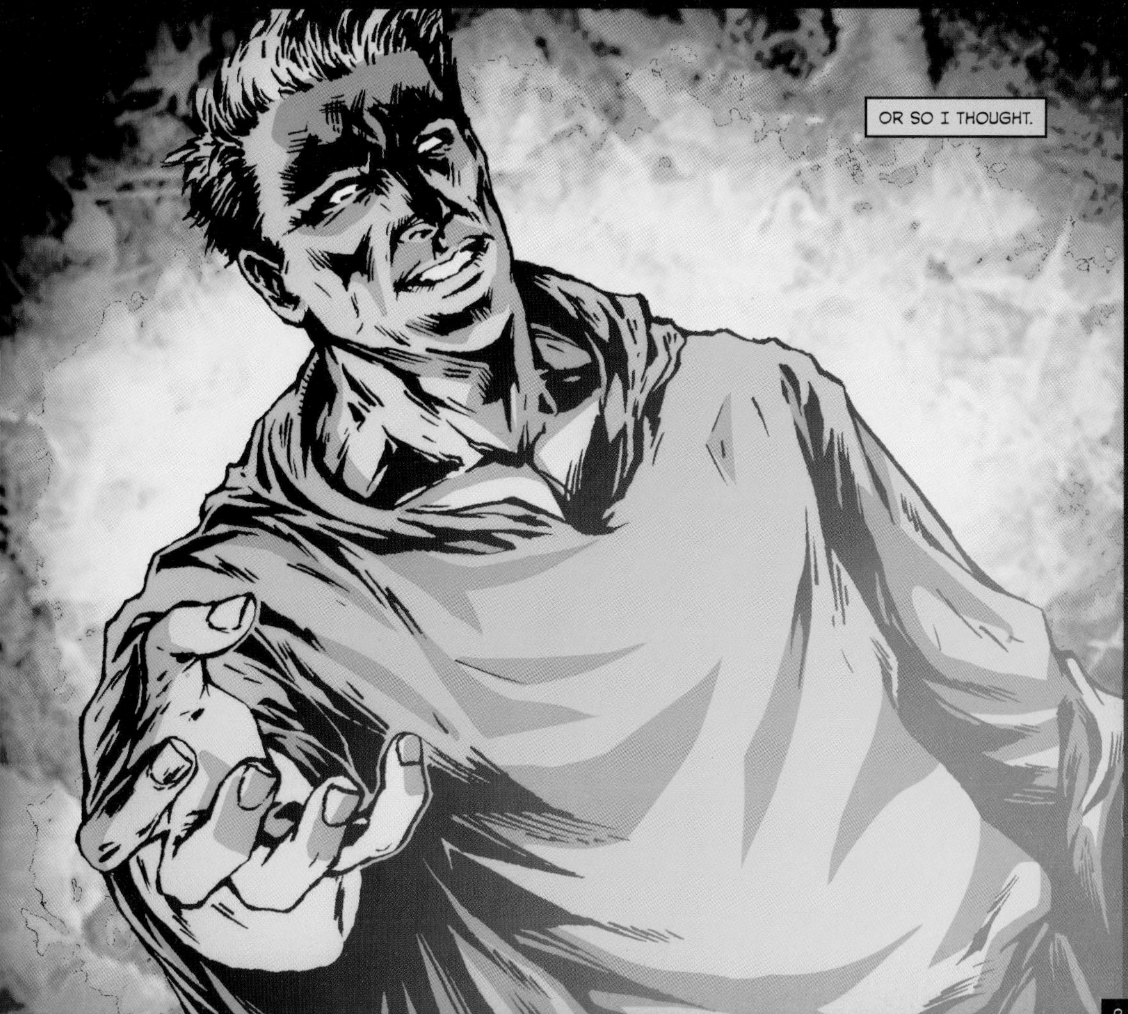
OR SO I THOUGHT.

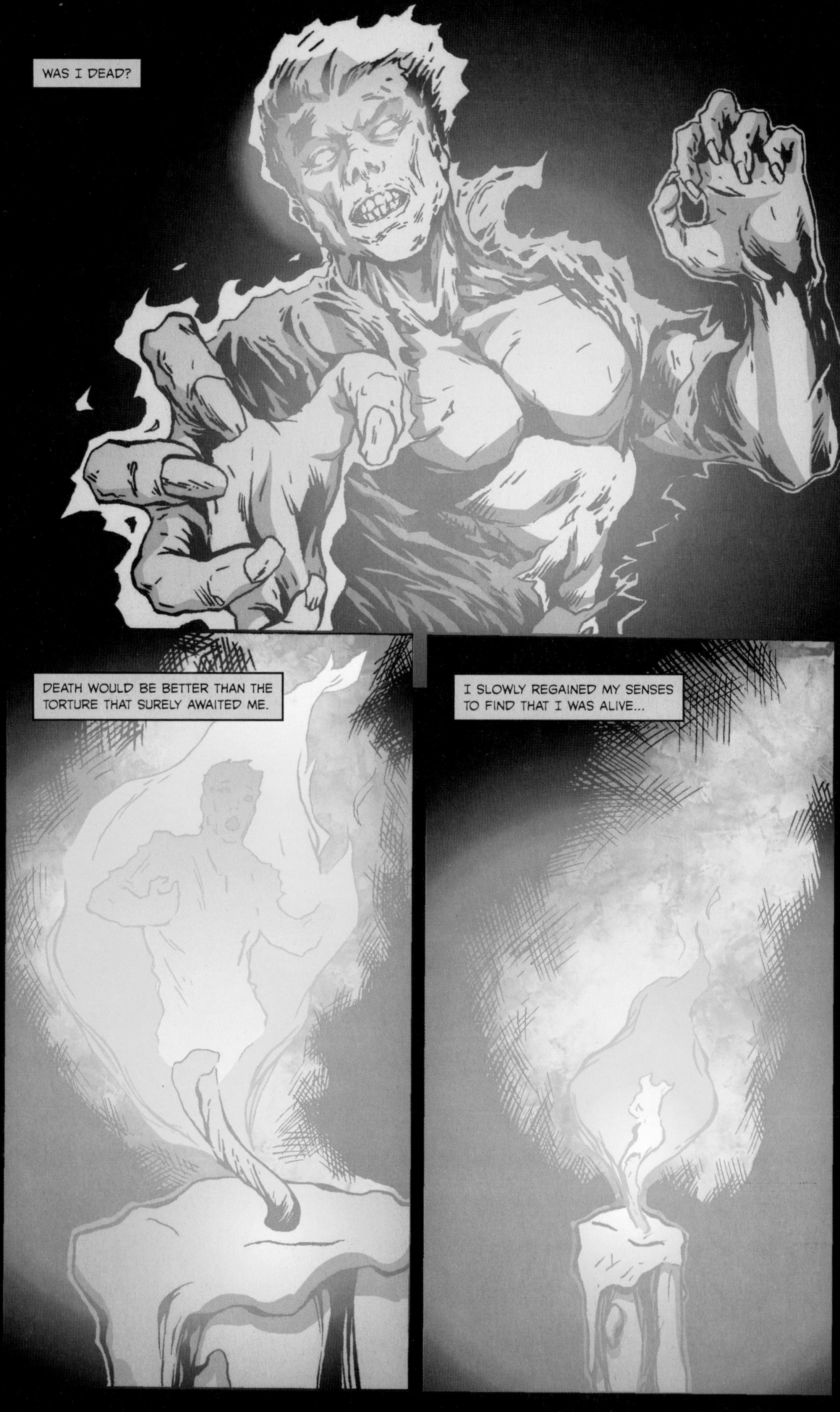
WAS I DEAD?
DEATH WOULD BE BETTER THAN THE TORTURE THAT SURELY AWAITED ME.
I SLOWLY REGAINED MY SENSES TO FIND THAT I WAS ALIVE...

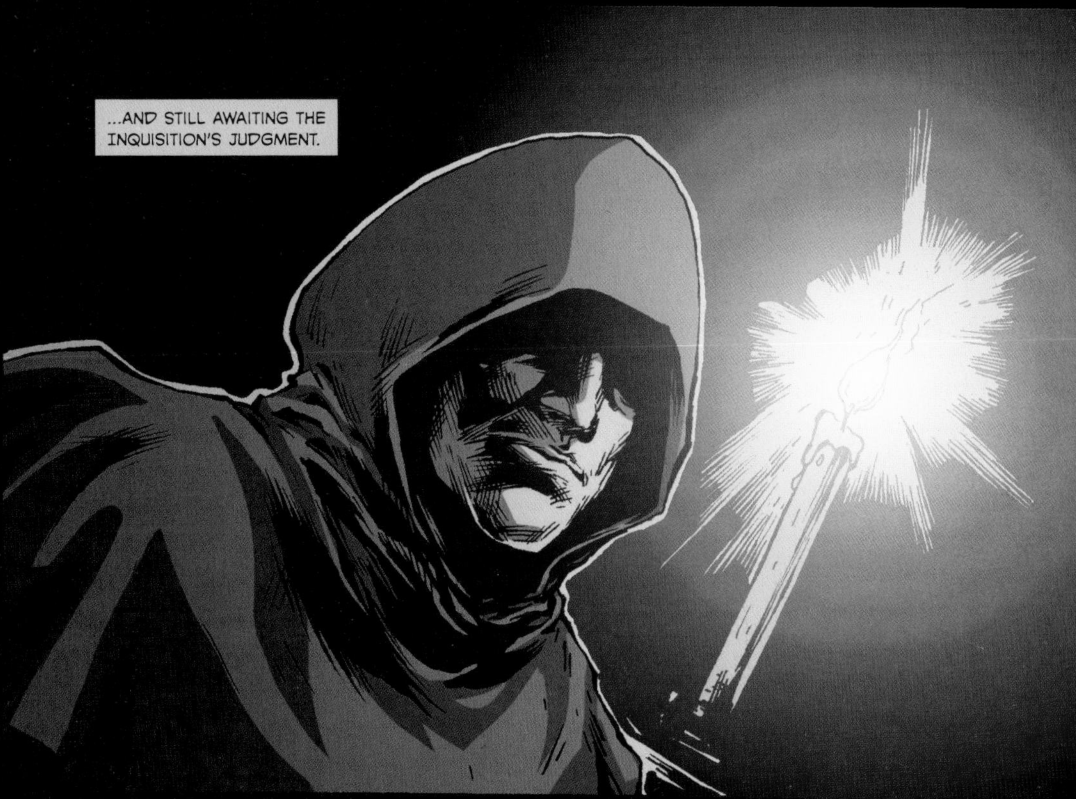
...AND STILL AWAITING THE INQUISITION'S JUDGMENT.

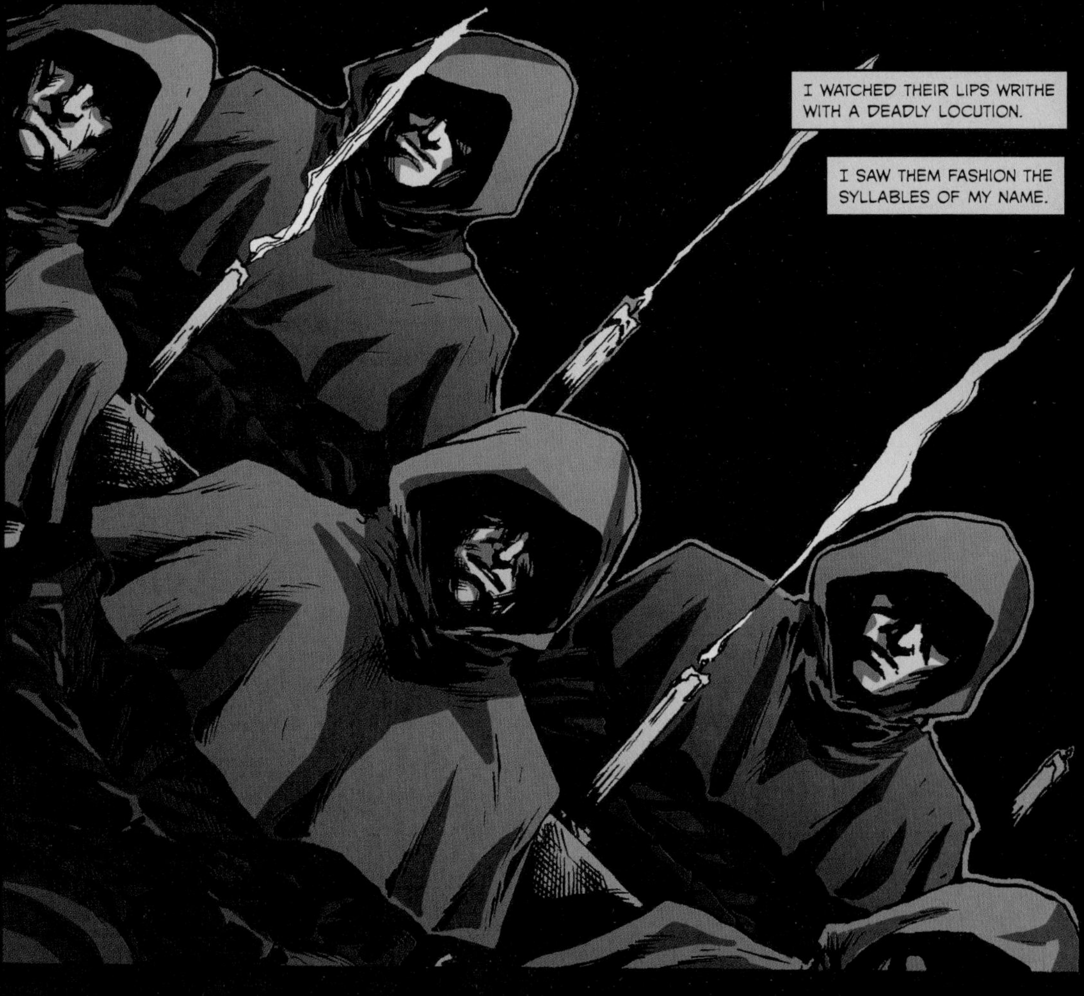
I WATCHED THEIR LIPS WRITHE WITH A DEADLY LOCUTION.
I SAW THEM FASHION THE SYLLABLES OF MY NAME.

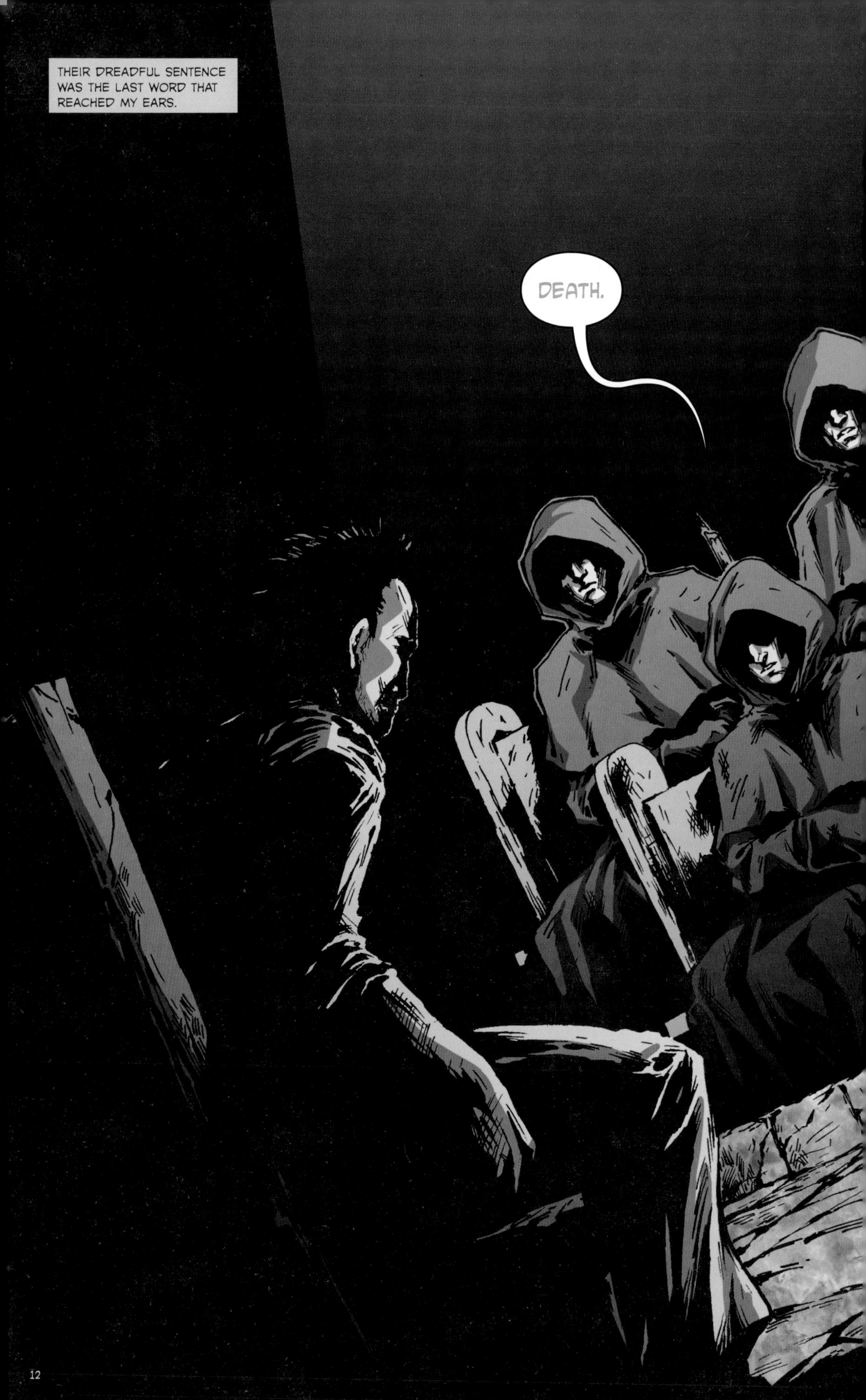
THEIR DREADFUL SENTENCE WAS THE LAST WORD THAT REACHED MY EARS.
DEATH.

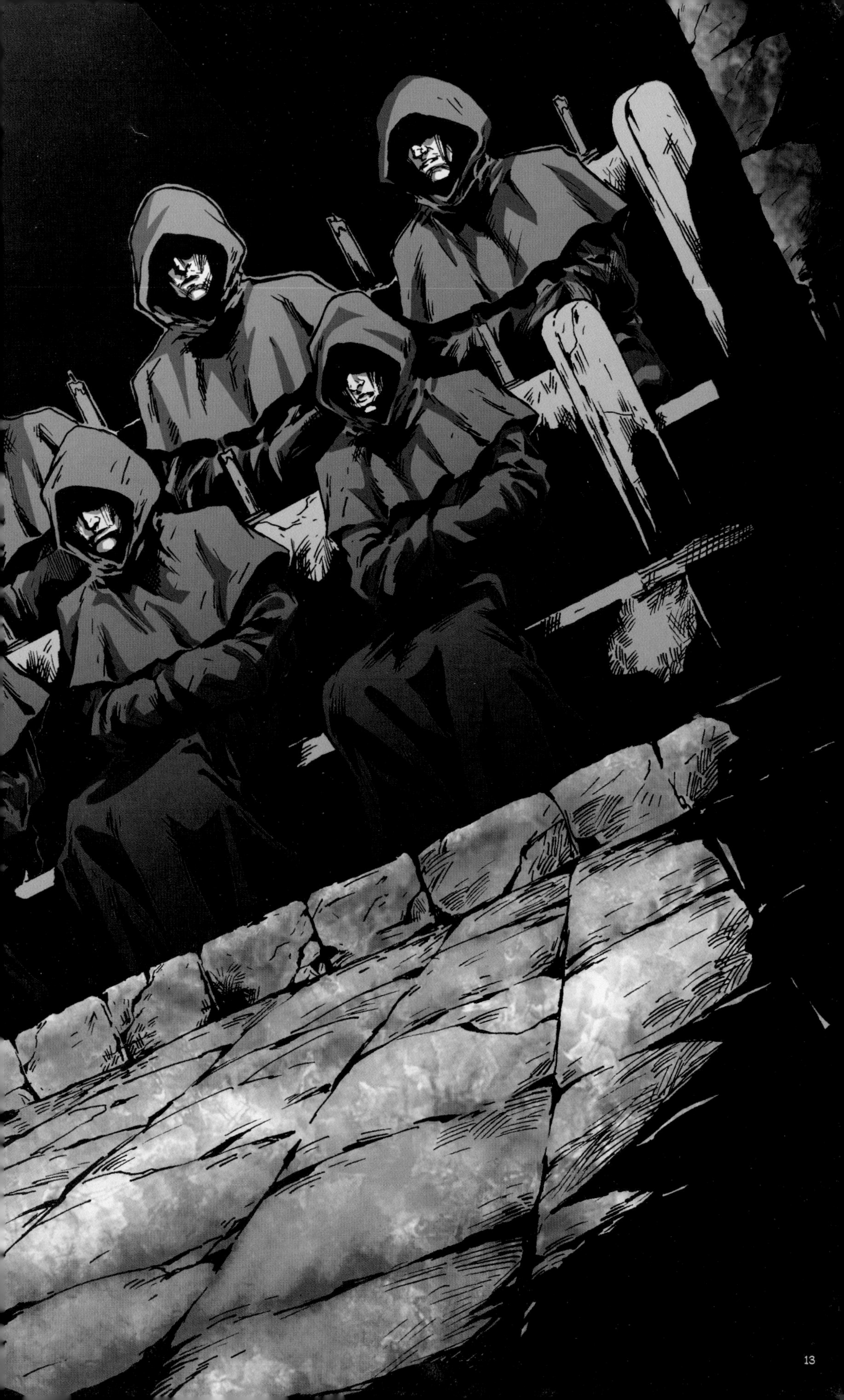

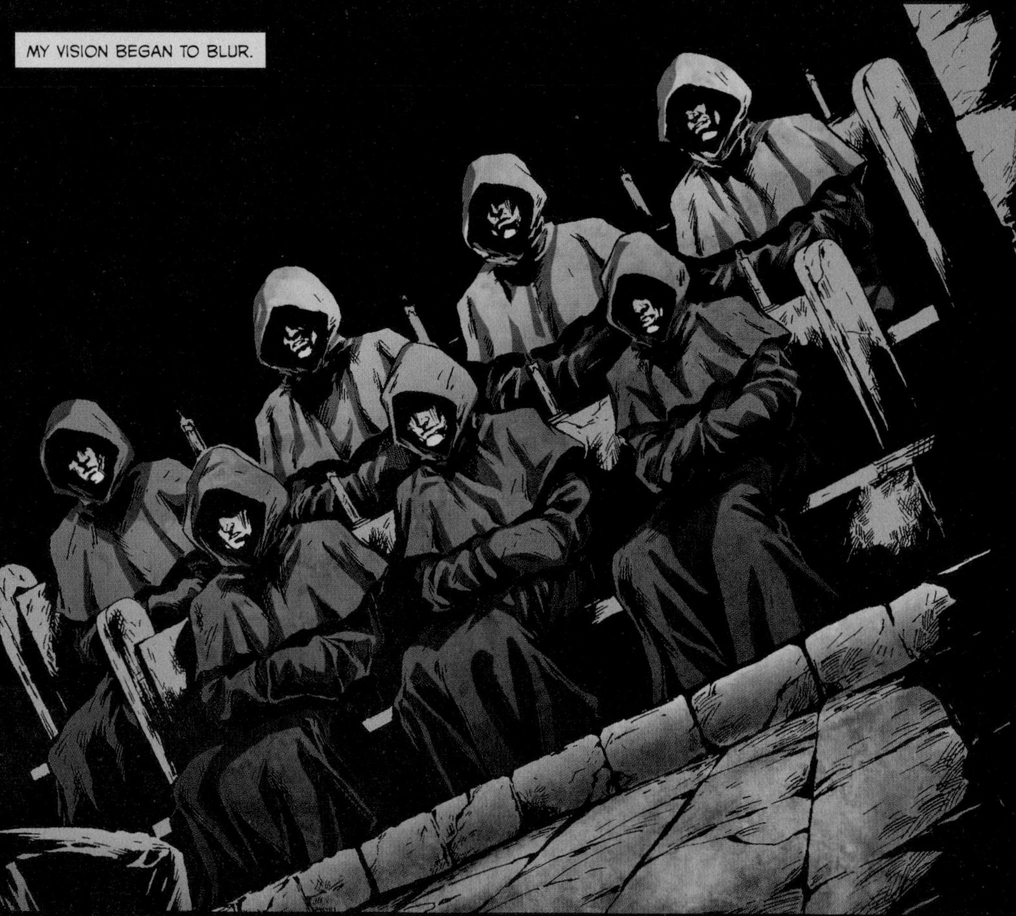
MY VISION BEGAN TO BLUR.

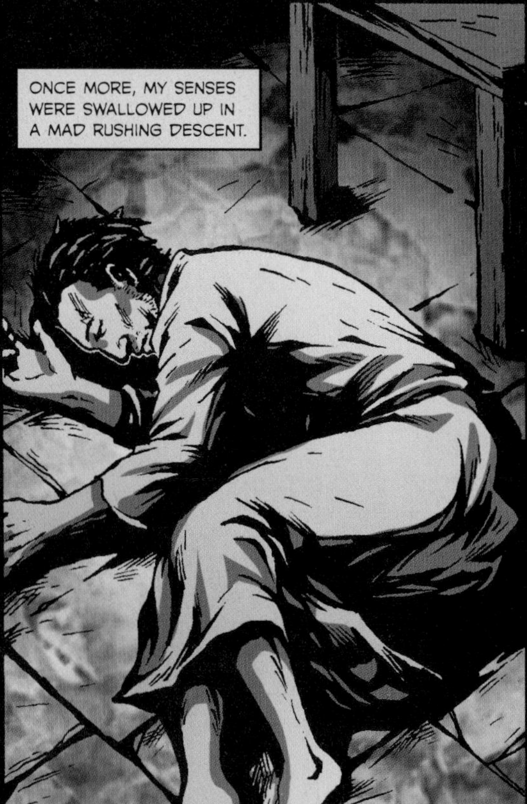
ONCE MORE, MY SENSES WERE SWALLOWED UP IN A MAD RUSHING DESCENT.

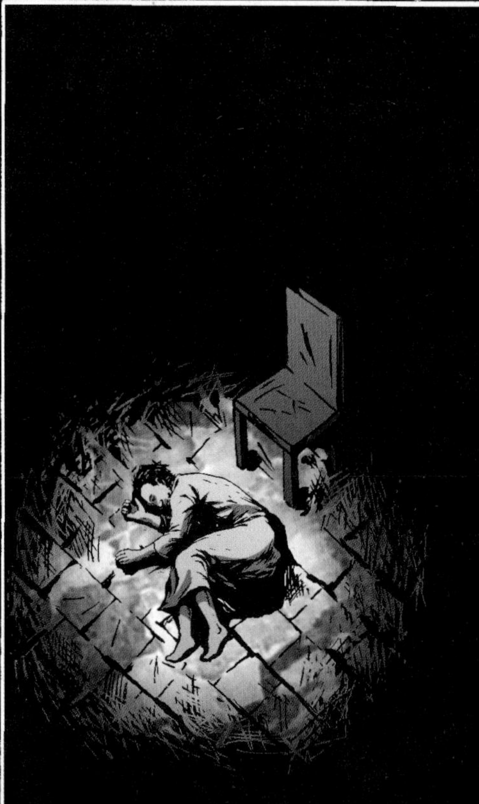

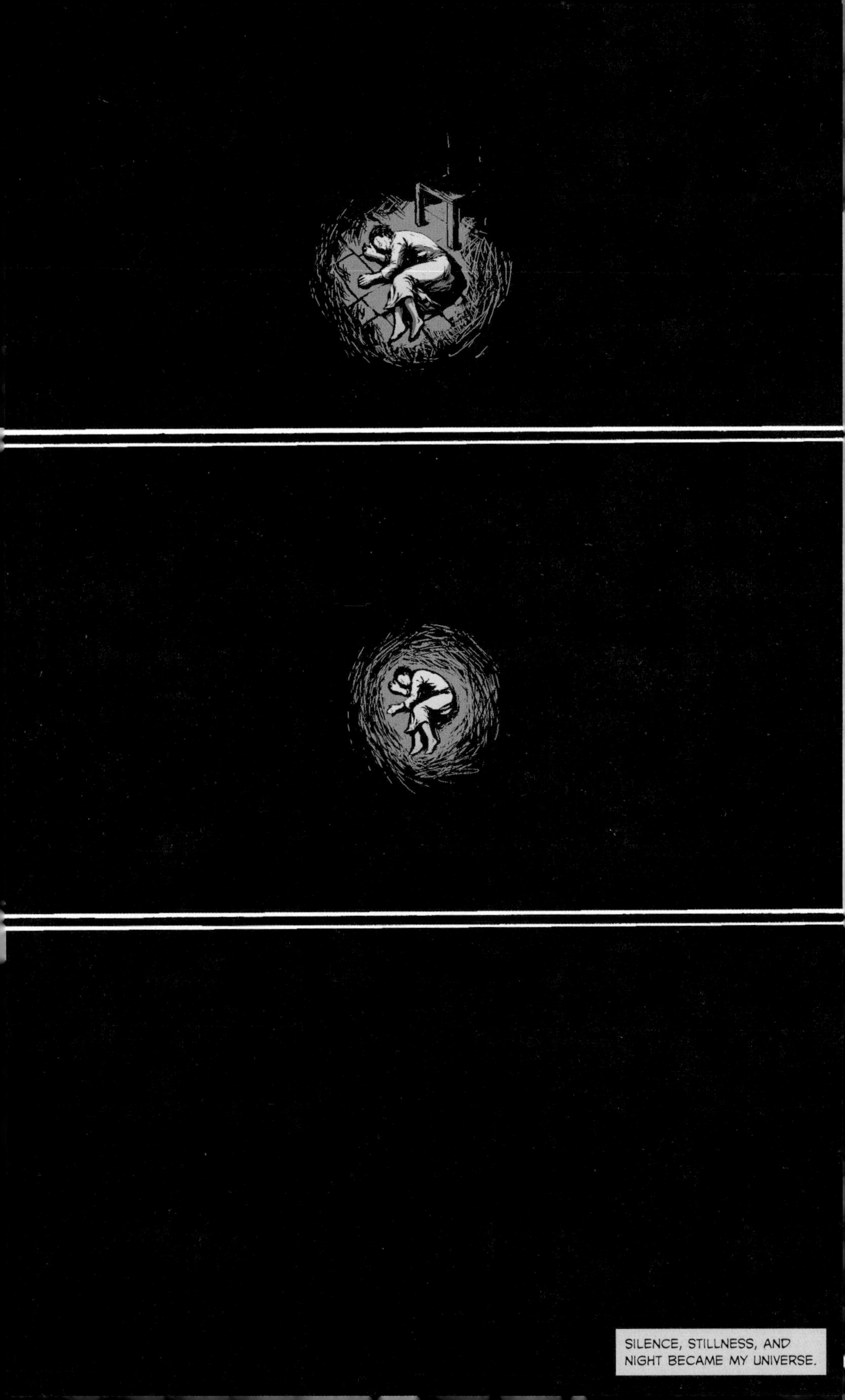
SILENCE, STILLNESS, AND NIGHT BECAME MY UNIVERSE.

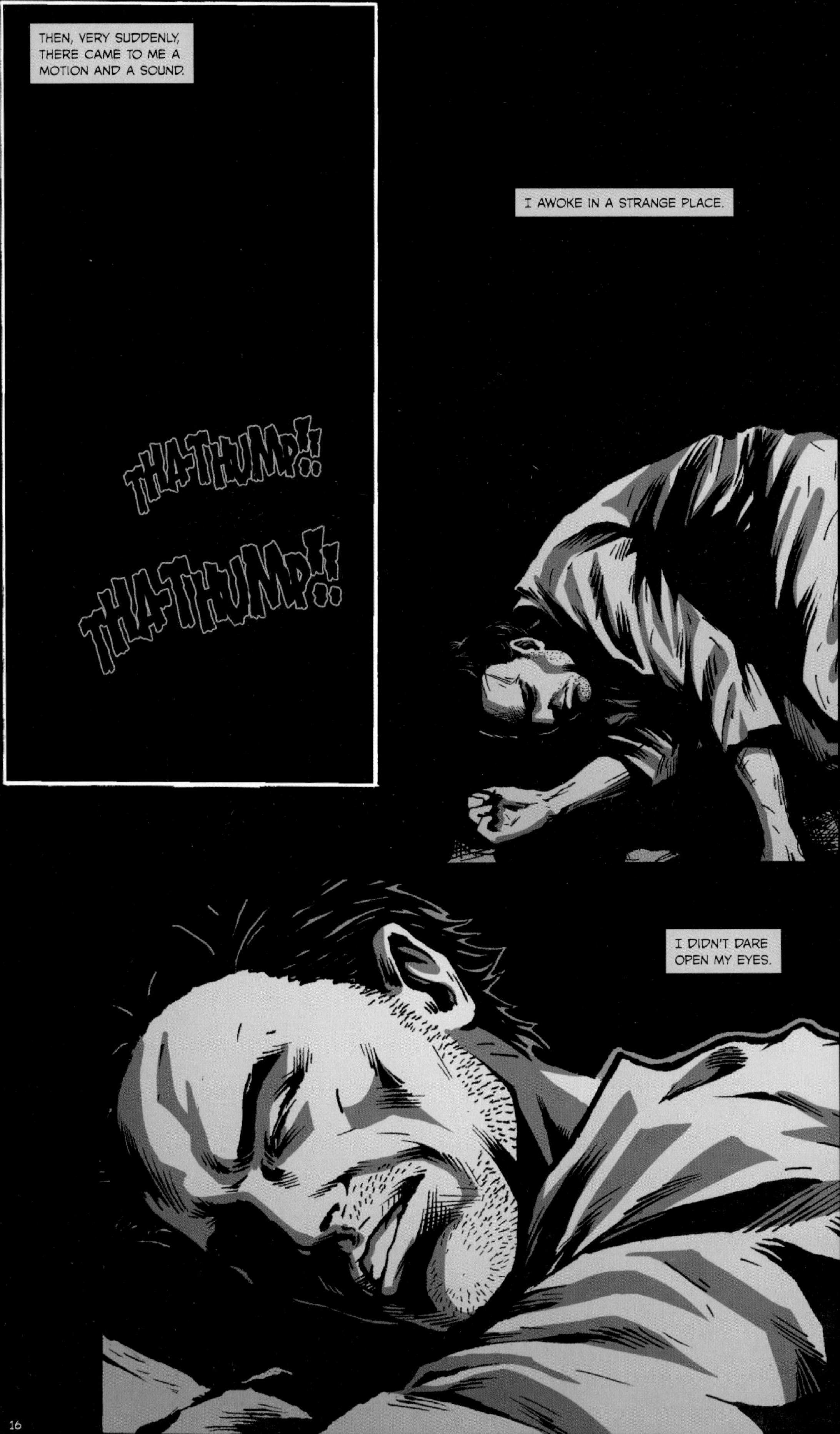
THEN, VERY SUDDENLY, THERE CAME TO ME A MOTION AND A SOUND.
THATHUMP!!
THATHUMP!!
I AWOKE IN A STRANGE PLACE.
I DIDN'T DARE OPEN MY EYES.

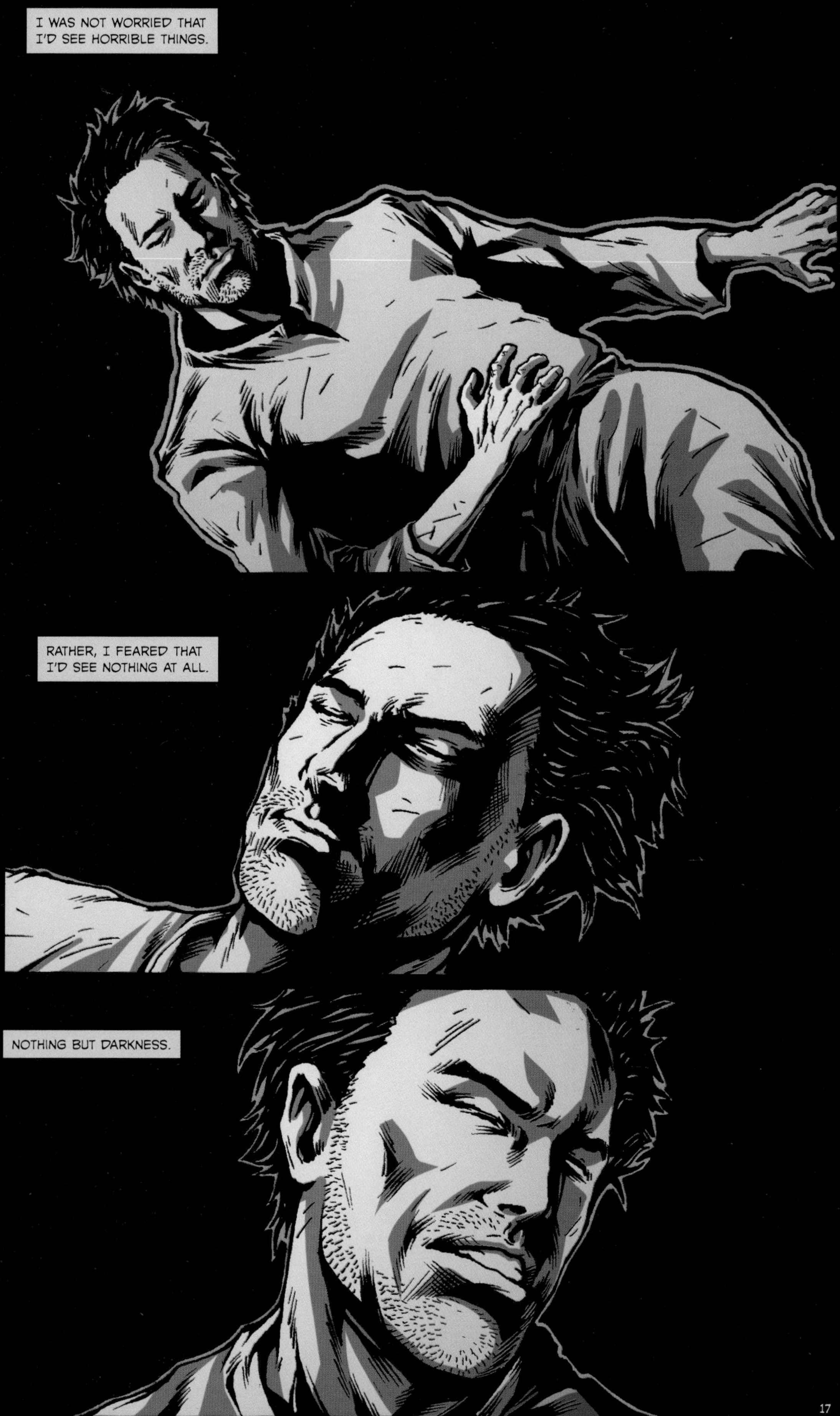
I WAS NOT WORRIED THAT I'D SEE HORRIBLE THINGS.
RATHER, I FEARED THAT I'D SEE NOTHING AT ALL.
NOTHING BUT DARKNESS.

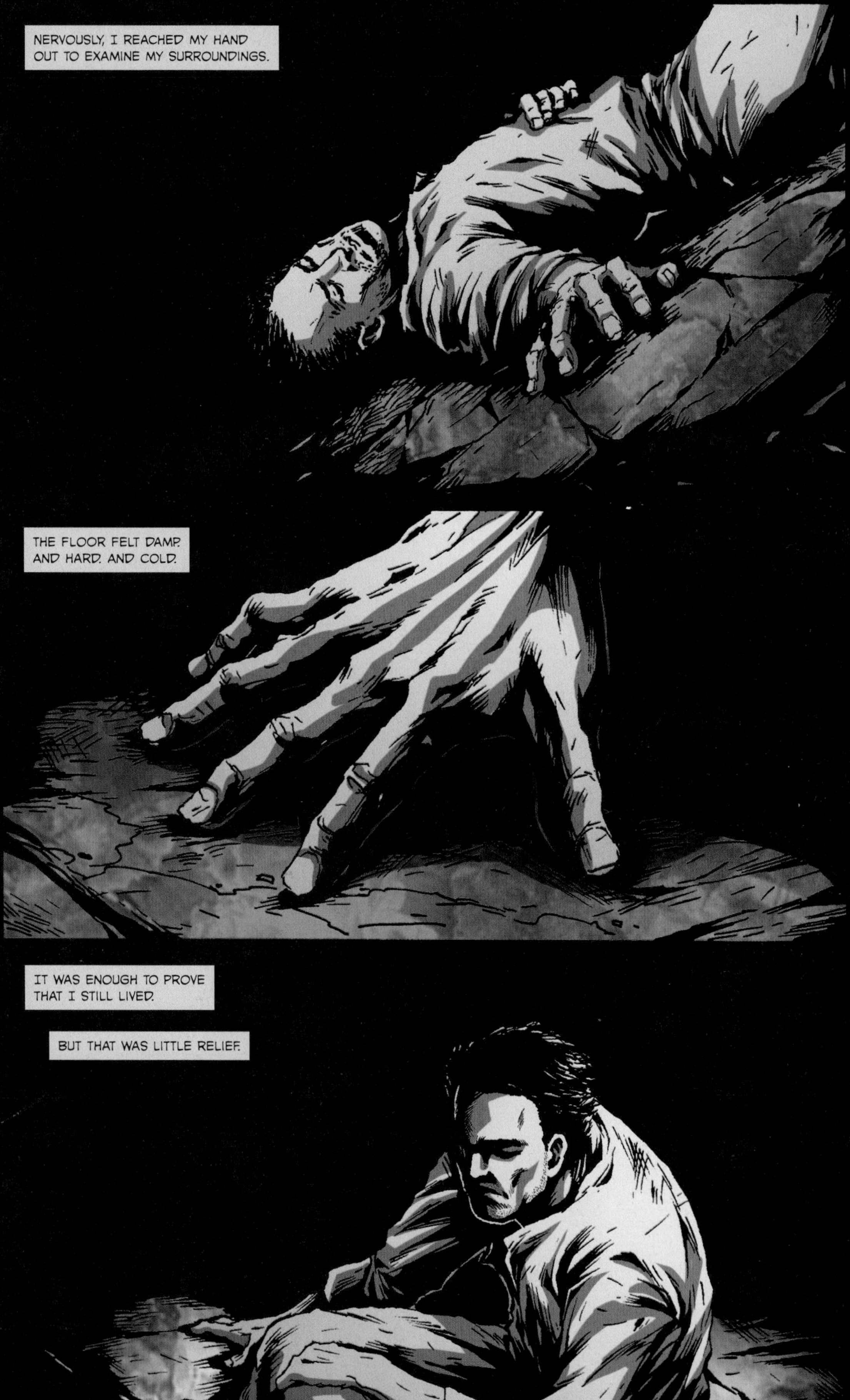
NERVOUSLY, I REACHED MY HAND OUT TO EXAMINE MY SURROUNDINGS.
THE FLOOR FELT DAMP. AND HARD. AND COLD.
IT WAS ENOUGH TO PROVE THAT I STILL LIVED.
BUT THAT WAS LITTLE RELIEF.

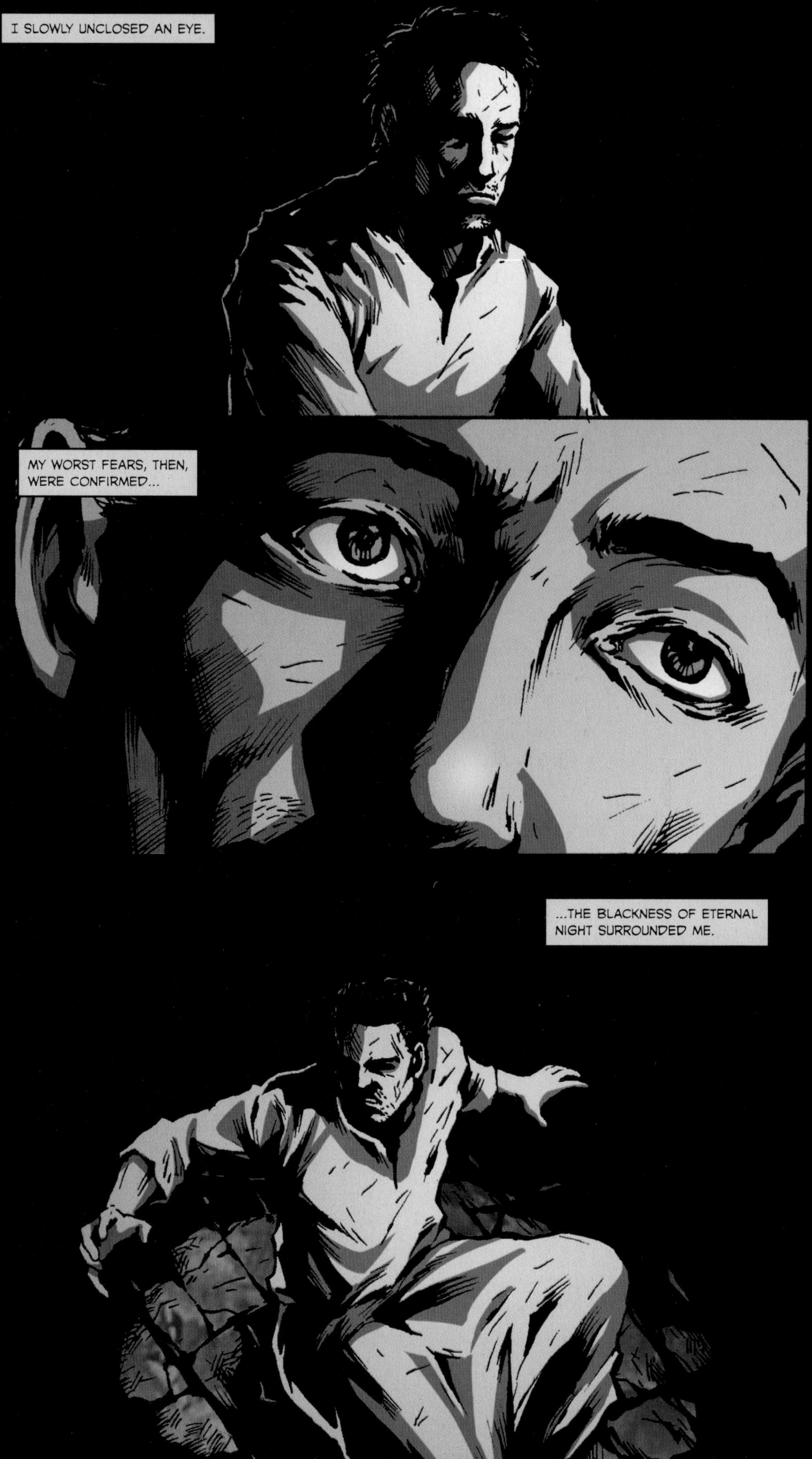
I SLOWLY UNCLOSED AN EYE.
MY WORST FEARS, THEN, WERE CONFIRMED...
...THE BLACKNESS OF ETERNAL NIGHT SURROUNDED ME.

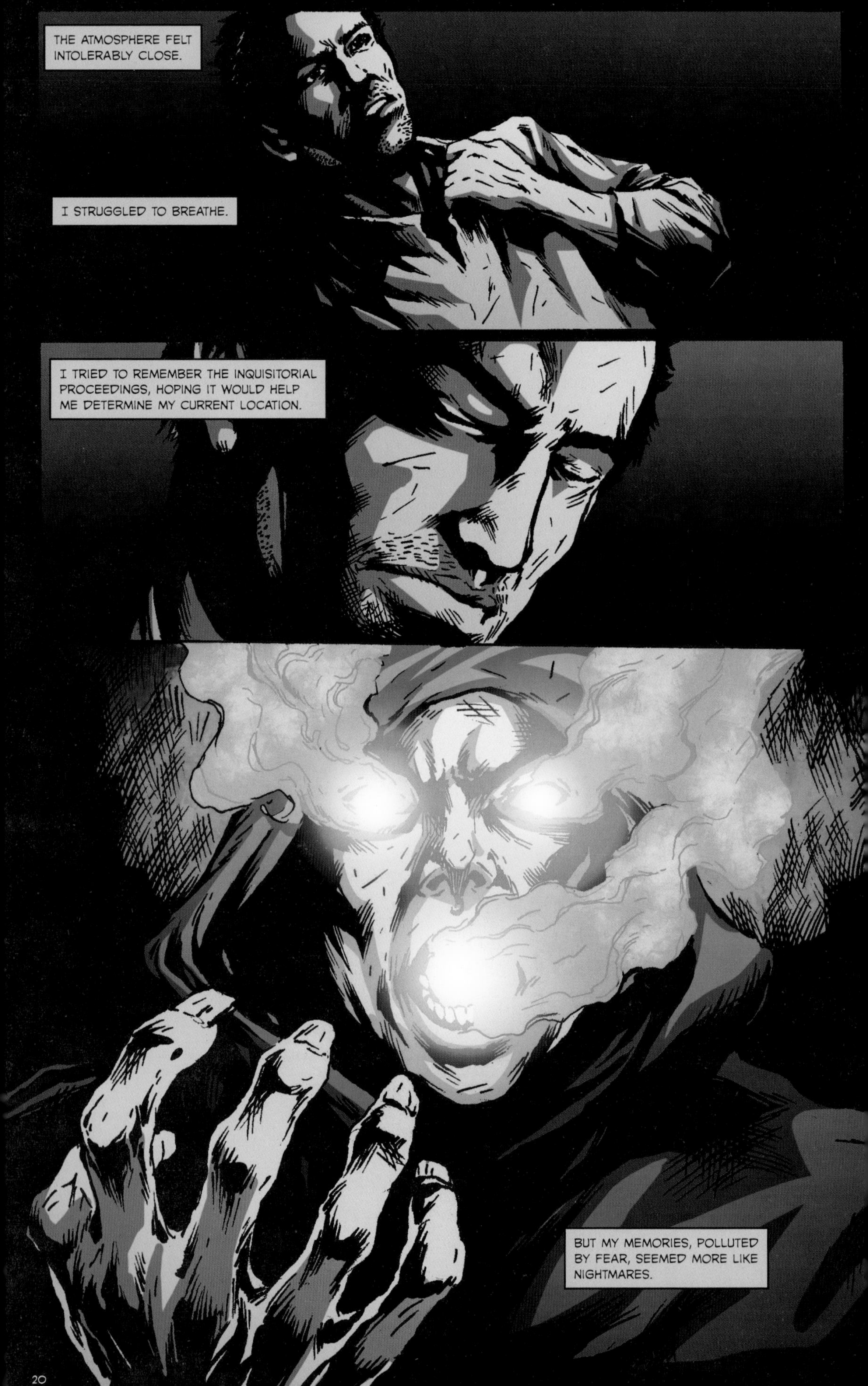
THE ATMOSPHERE FELT INTOLERABLY CLOSE.
I STRUGGLED TO BREATHE.
I TRIED TO REMEMBER THE INQUISITORIAL PROCEEDINGS, HOPING IT WOULD HELP ME DETERMINE MY CURRENT LOCATION.
BUT MY MEMORIES, POLLUTED BY FEAR, SEEMED MORE LIKE NIGHTMARES.

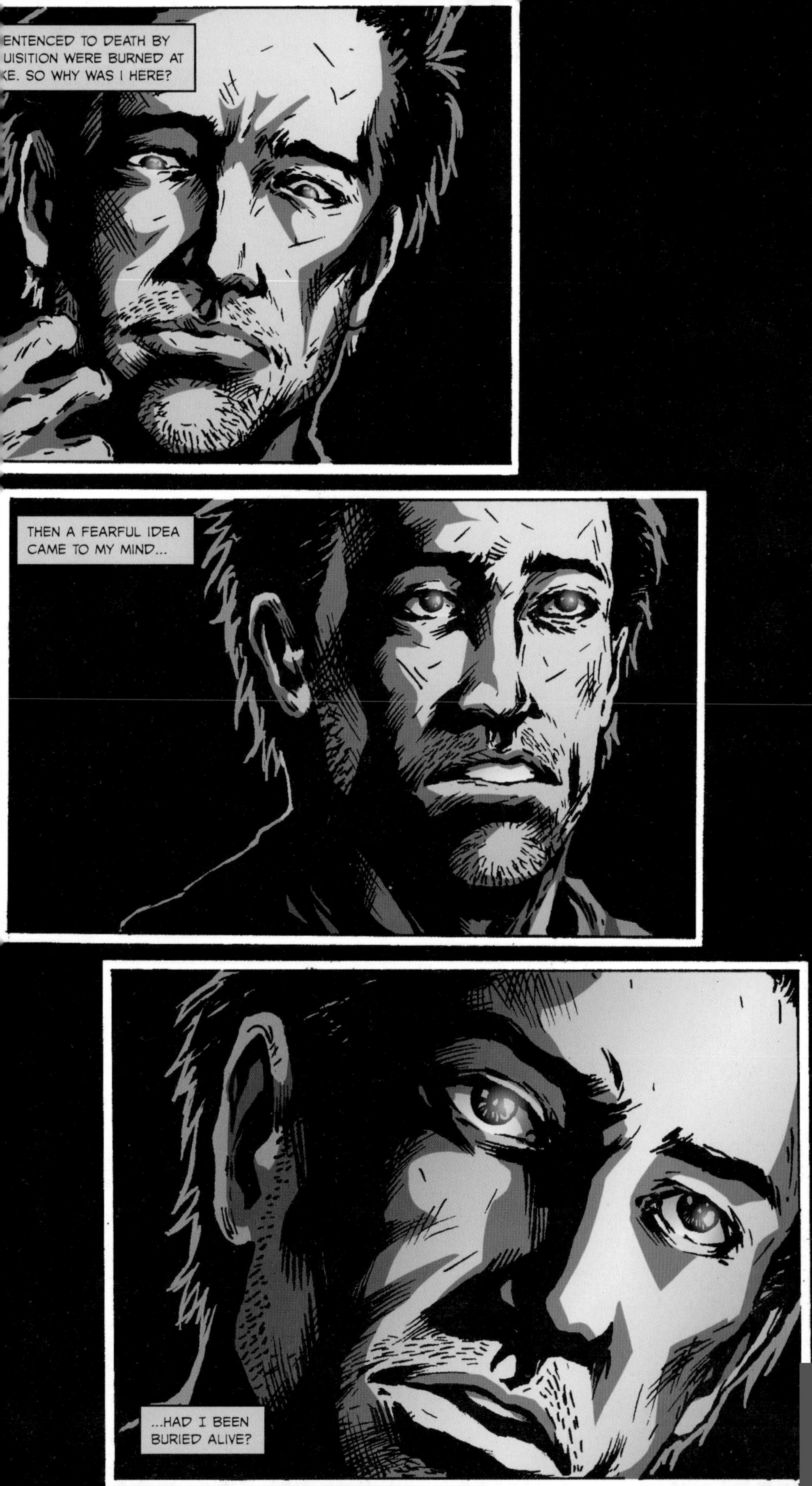
ENTENCED TO DEATH BY
UISITION WERE BURNED AT
KE. SO WHY WAS I HERE?
THEN A FEARFUL IDEA
CAME TO MY MIND...
...HAD I BEEN
BURIED ALIVE?

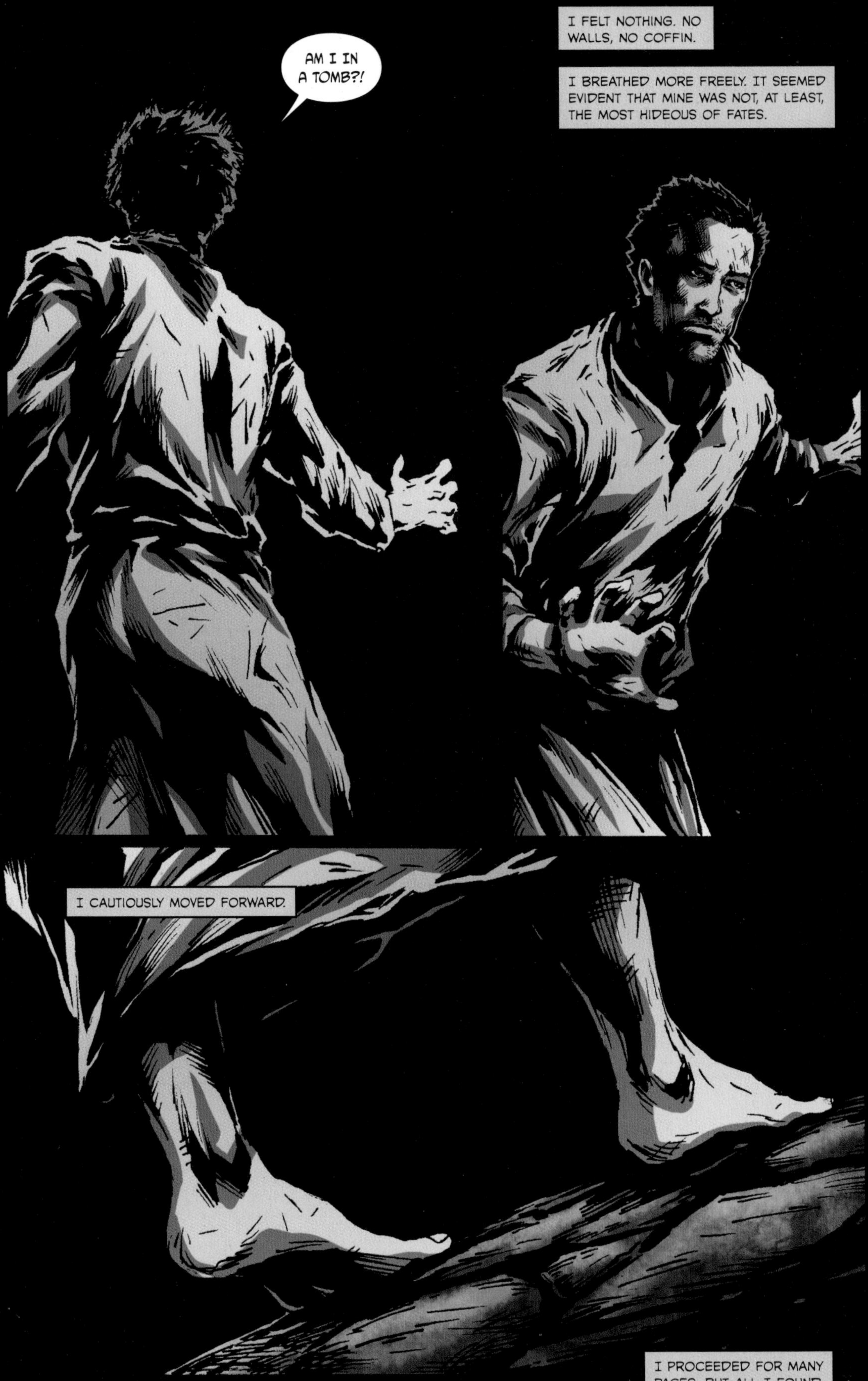
AM I IN A TOMB?!
I FELT NOTHING. NO WALLS, NO COFFIN.
I BREATHED MORE FREELY. IT SEEMED EVIDENT THAT MINE WAS NOT, AT LEAST, THE MOST HIDEOUS OF FATES.
I CAUTIOUSLY MOVED FORWARD.
I PROCEEDED FOR MANY PACES, BUT ALL I FOUND WAS BLACKNESS.

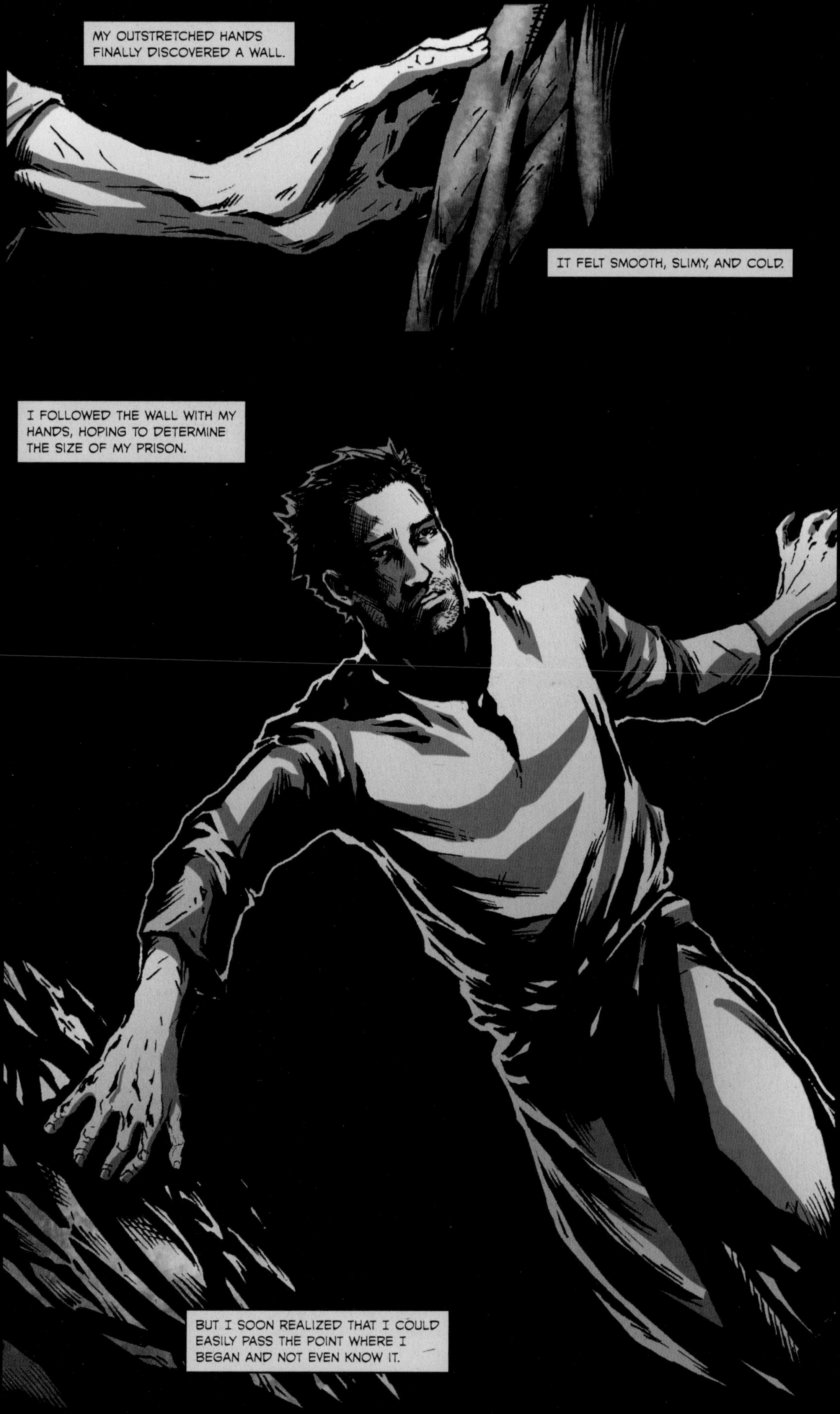
MY OUTSTRETCHED HANDS FINALLY DISCOVERED A WALL.
IT FELT SMOOTH, SLIMY, AND COLD.
I FOLLOWED THE WALL WITH MY HANDS, HOPING TO DETERMINE THE SIZE OF MY PRISON.
BUT I SOON REALIZED THAT I COULD EASILY PASS THE POINT WHERE I BEGAN AND NOT EVEN KNOW IT.

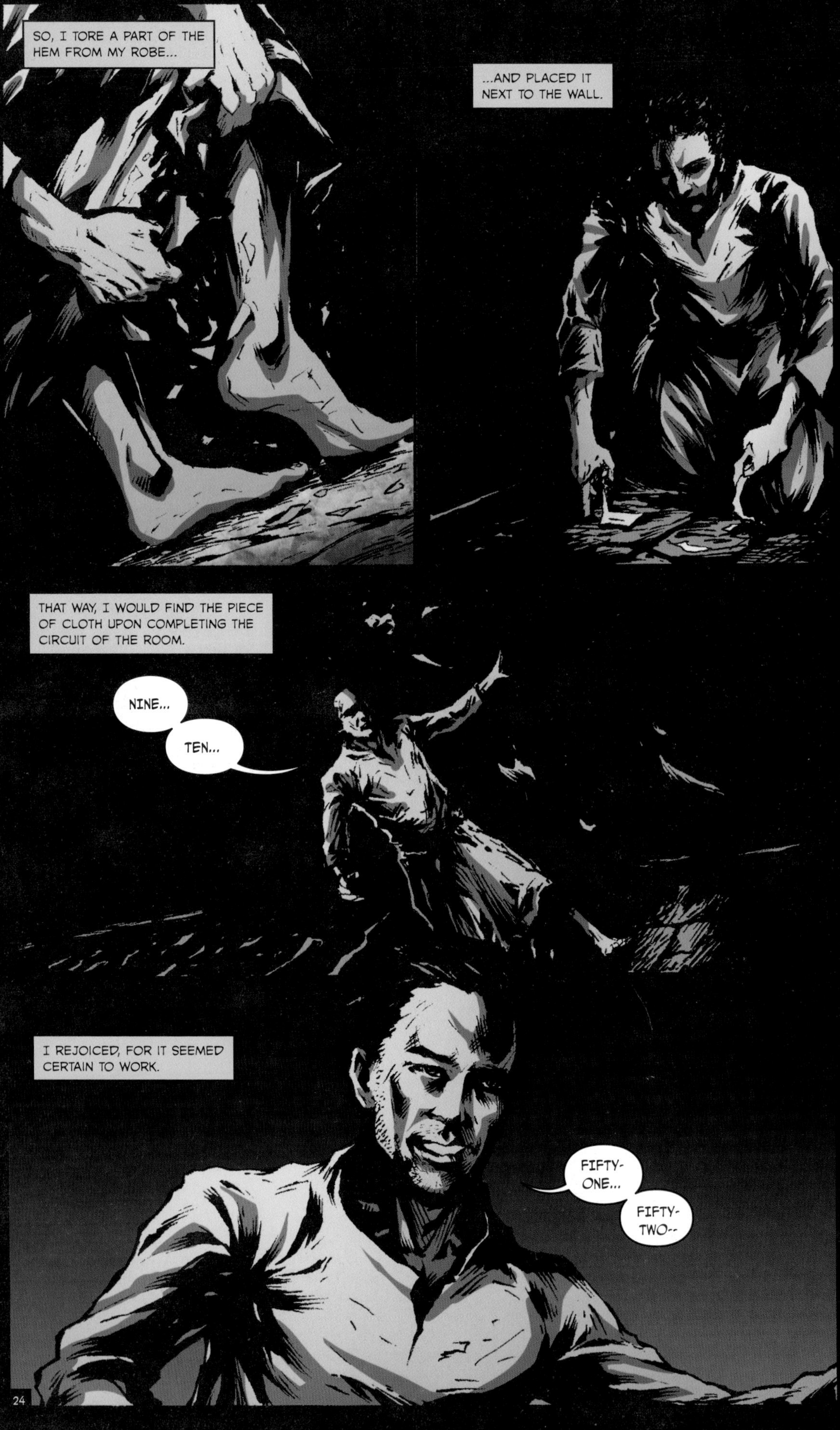
SO, I TORE A PART OF THE HEM FROM MY ROBE...
...AND PLACED IT NEXT TO THE WALL.
THAT WAY, I WOULD FIND THE PIECE OF CLOTH UPON COMPLETING THE CIRCUIT OF THE ROOM.
NINE...
TEN...
I REJOICED, FOR IT SEEMED CERTAIN TO WORK.
FIFTY-ONE...
FIFTY-TWO--

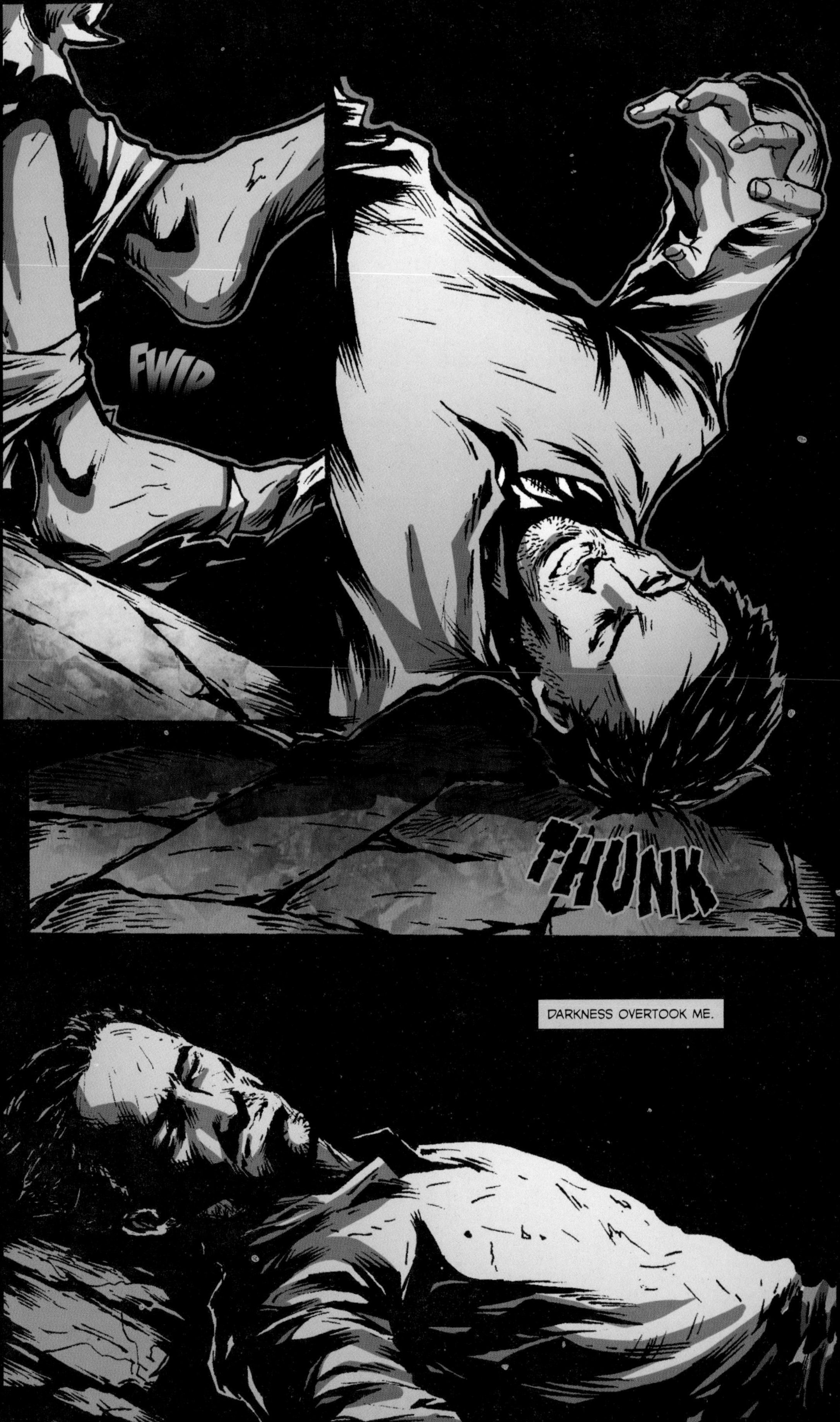
FWIP
THUNK
DARKNESS OVERTOOK ME.

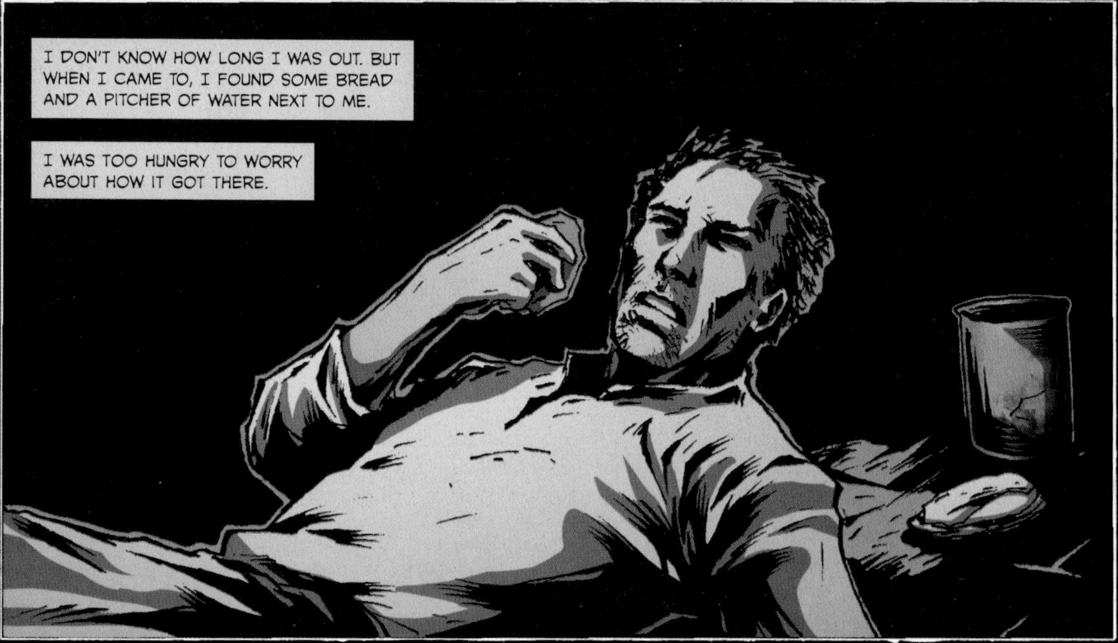
I DON'T KNOW HOW LONG I WAS OUT. BUT WHEN I CAME TO, I FOUND SOME BREAD AND A PITCHER OF WATER NEXT TO ME.
I WAS TOO HUNGRY TO WORRY ABOUT HOW IT GOT THERE.

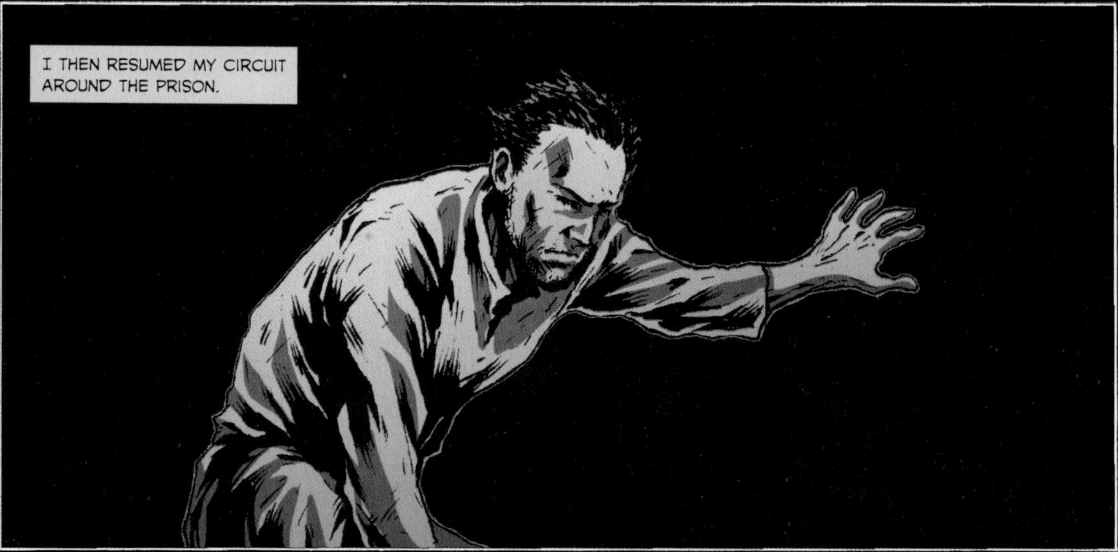
I THEN RESUMED MY CIRCUIT AROUND THE PRISON.

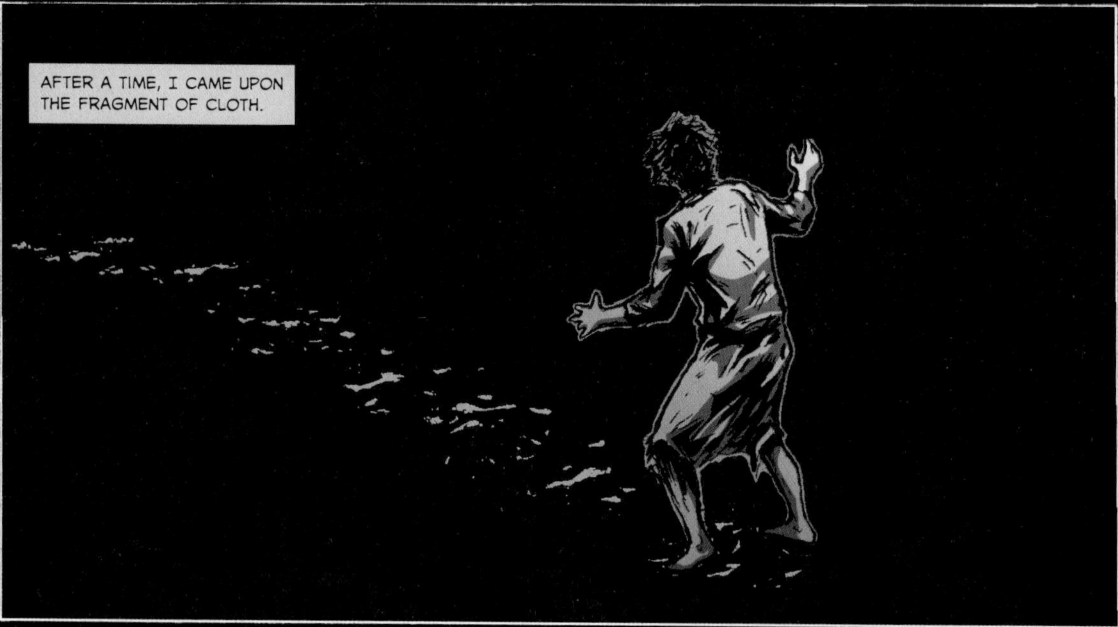
AFTER A TIME, I CAME UPON THE FRAGMENT OF CLOTH.

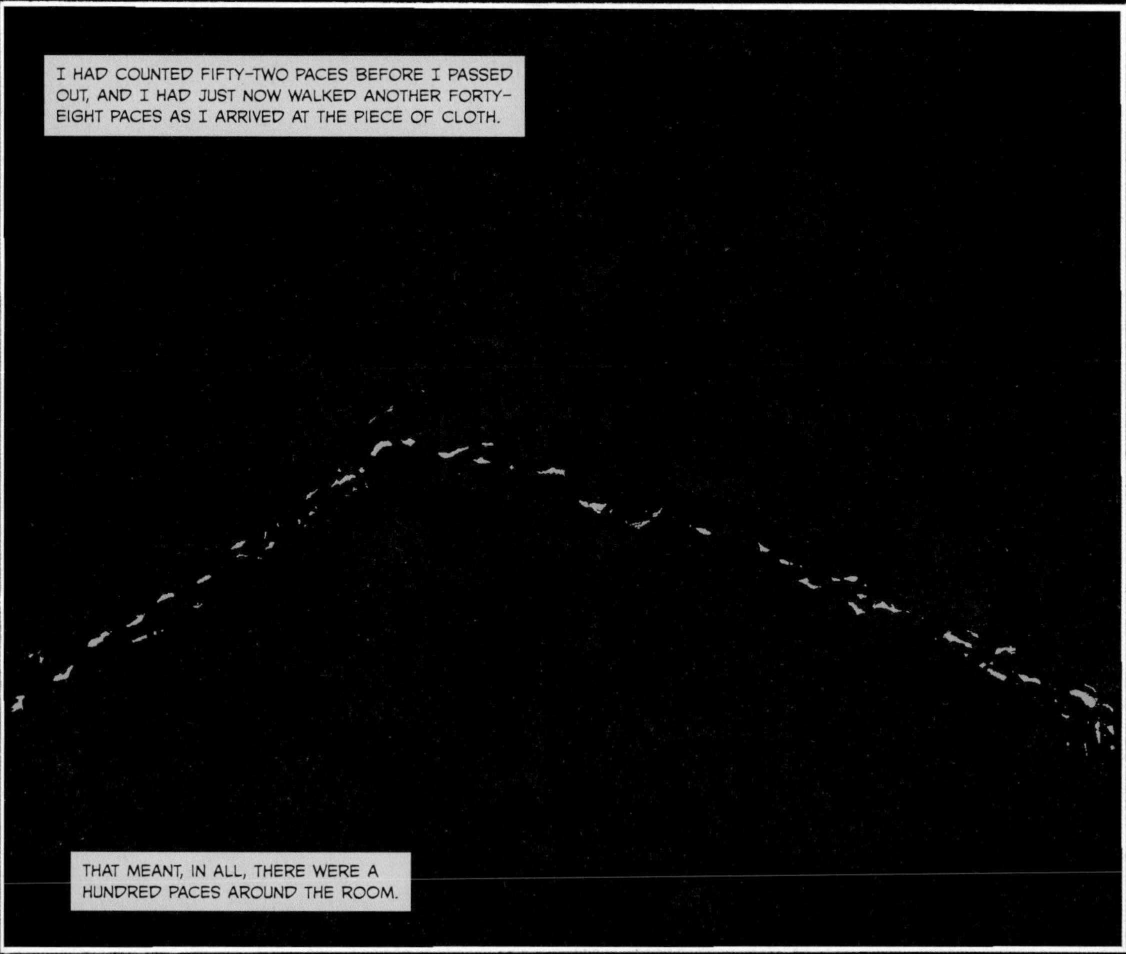
I HAD COUNTED FIFTY-TWO PACES BEFORE I PASSED OUT, AND I HAD JUST NOW WALKED ANOTHER FORTY-EIGHT PACES AS I ARRIVED AT THE PIECE OF CLOTH.
THAT MEANT, IN ALL, THERE WERE A HUNDRED PACES AROUND THE ROOM.

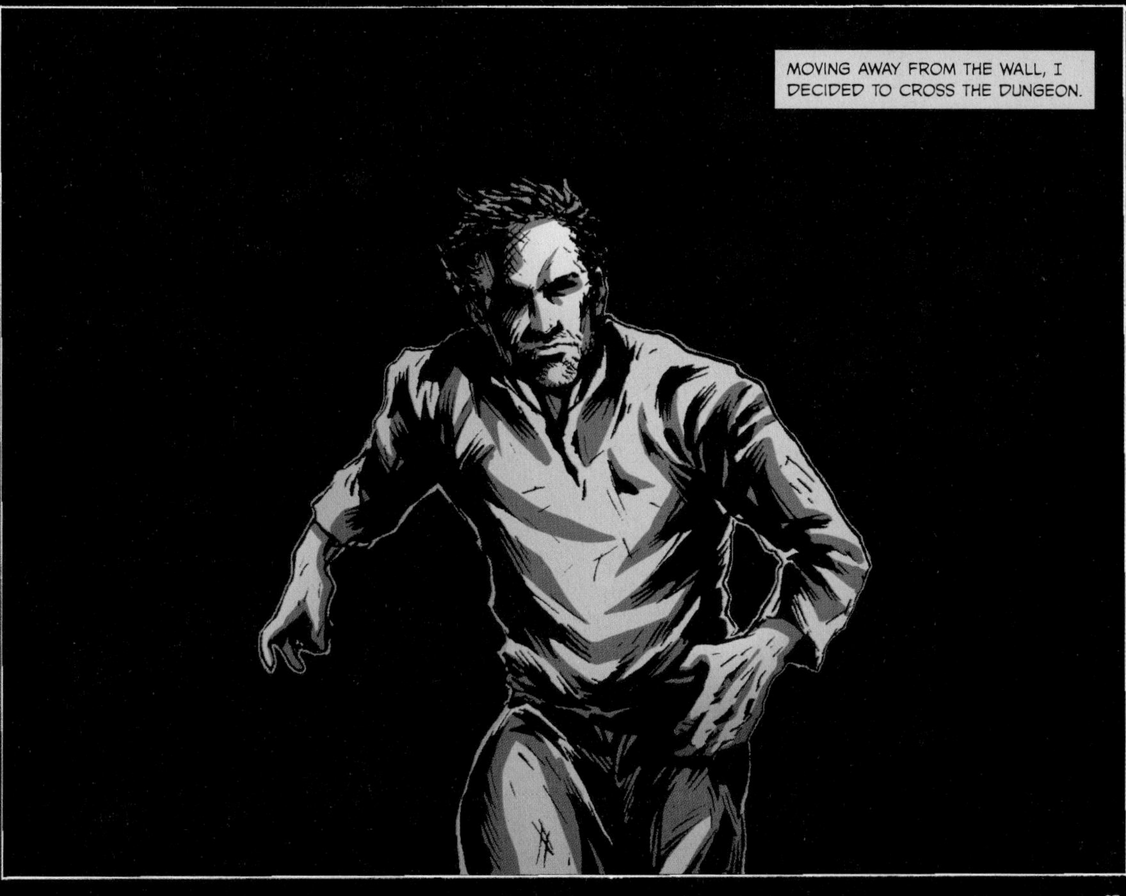
MOVING AWAY FROM THE WALL, I DECIDED TO CROSS THE DUNGEON.

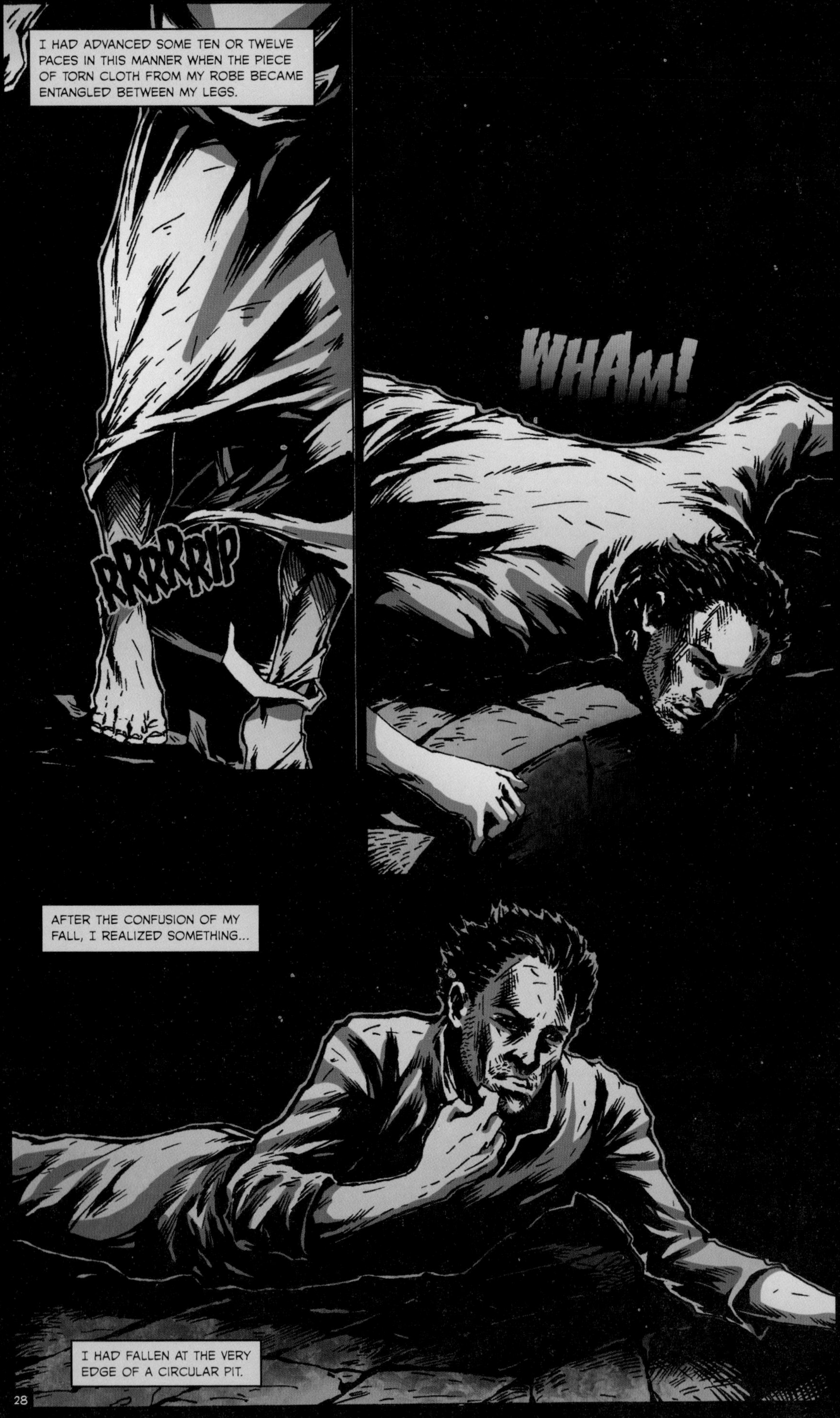
I HAD ADVANCED SOME TEN OR TWELVE PACES IN THIS MANNER WHEN THE PIECE OF TORN CLOTH FROM MY ROBE BECAME ENTANGLED BETWEEN MY LEGS.
RRRRRIP
WHAM!
AFTER THE CONFUSION OF MY FALL, I REALIZED SOMETHING...
I HAD FALLEN AT THE VERY EDGE OF A CIRCULAR PIT.

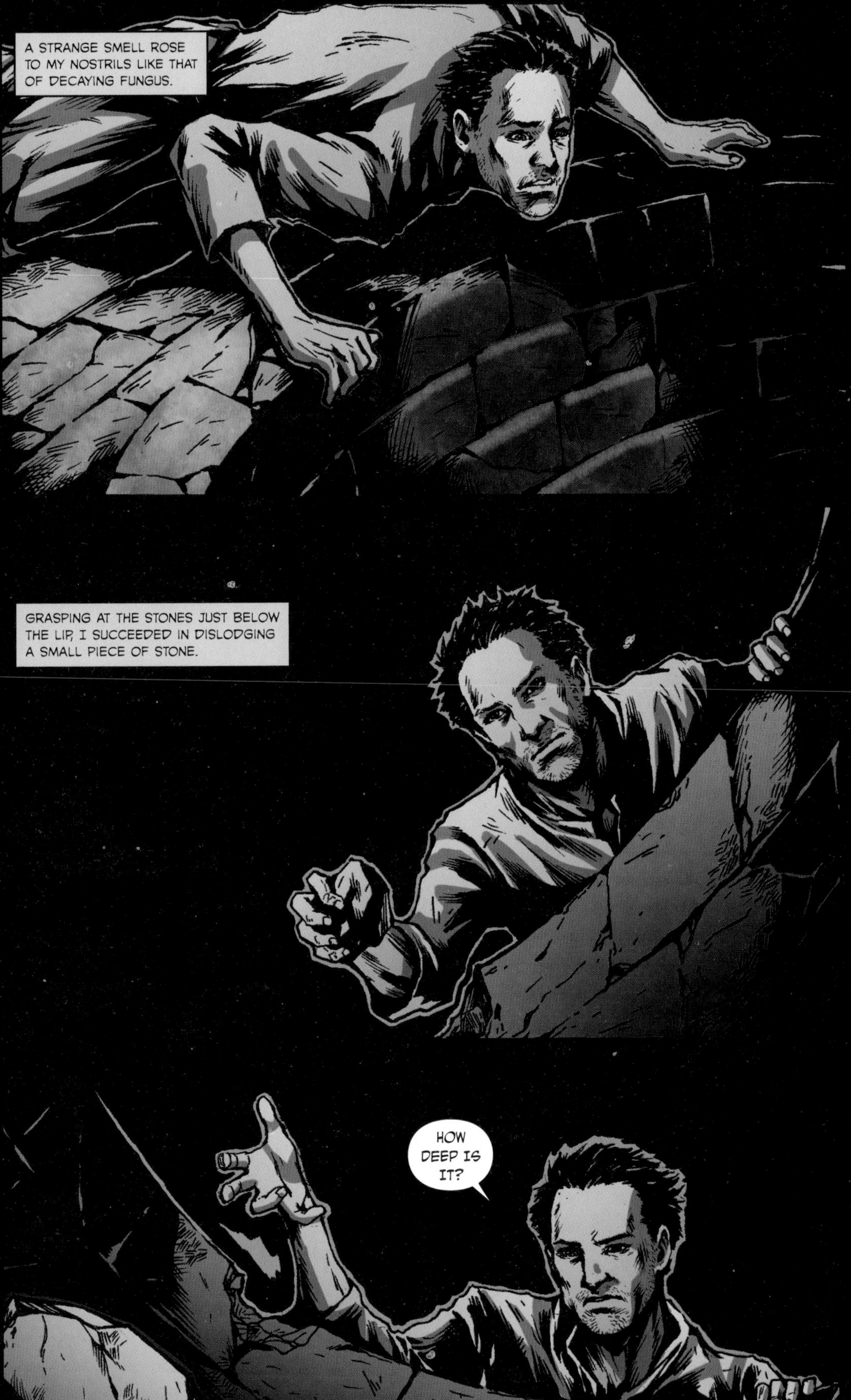
A STRANGE SMELL ROSE TO MY NOSTRILS LIKE THAT OF DECAYING FUNGUS.
GRASPING AT THE STONES JUST BELOW THE LIP, I SUCCEEDED IN DISLODGING A SMALL PIECE OF STONE.
HOW DEEP IS IT?

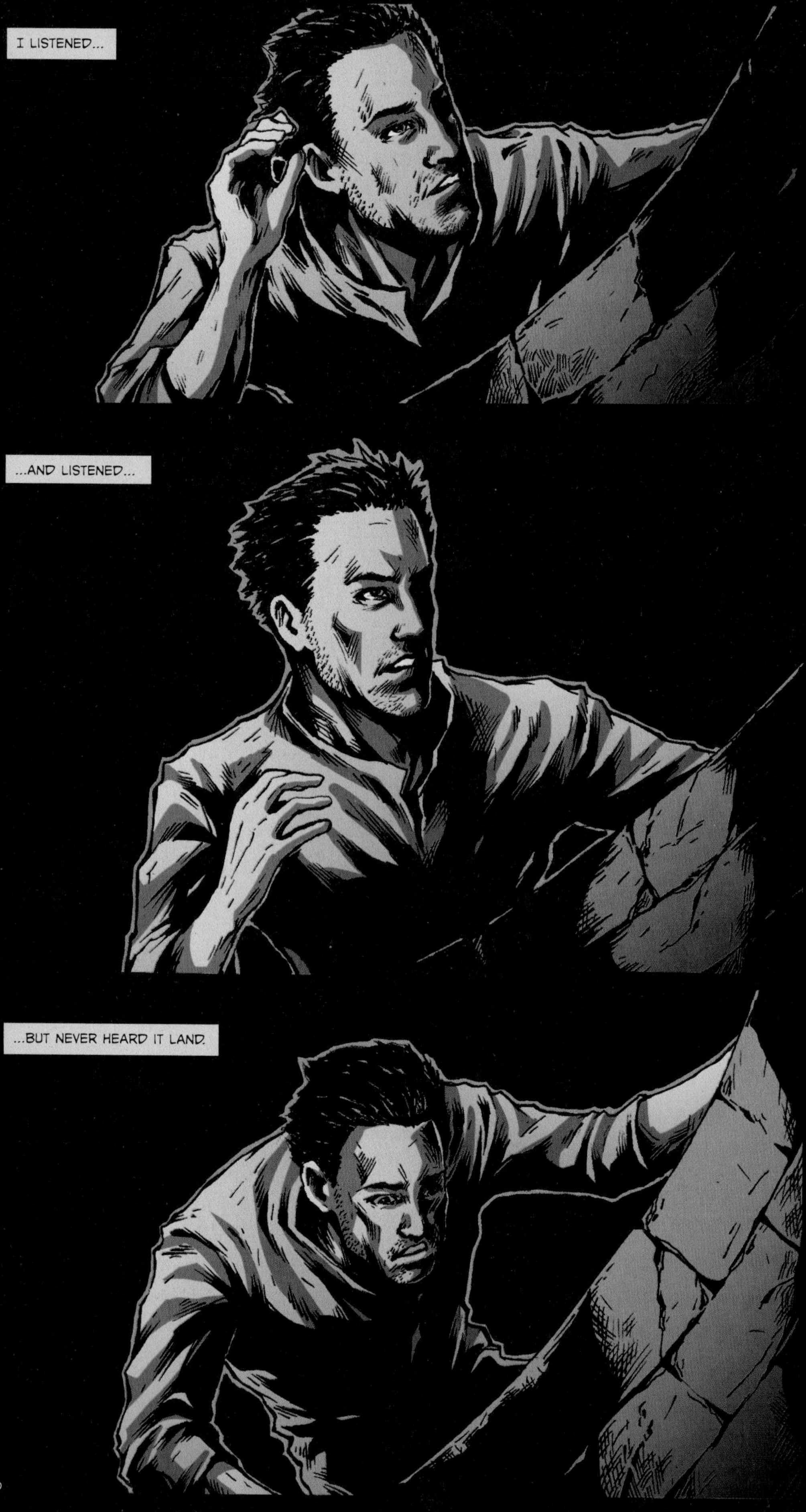
I LISTENED...
...AND LISTENED...
...BUT NEVER HEARD IT LAND.

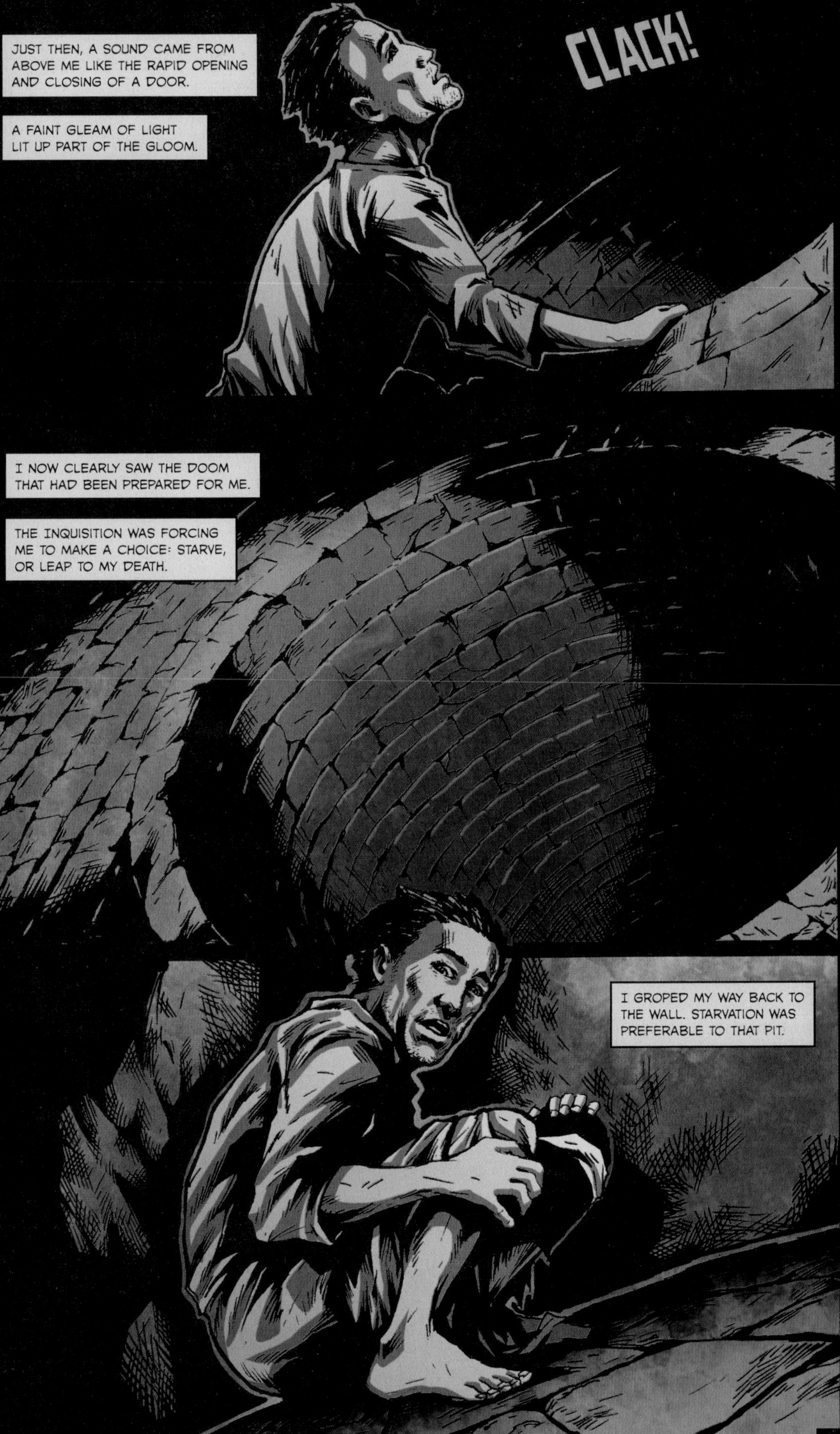
JUST THEN, A SOUND CAME FROM ABOVE ME LIKE THE RAPID OPENING AND CLOSING OF A DOOR.
CLACK!
A FAINT GLEAM OF LIGHT LIT UP PART OF THE GLOOM.
I NOW CLEARLY SAW THE DOOM THAT HAD BEEN PREPARED FOR ME.
THE INQUISITION WAS FORCING ME TO MAKE A CHOICE: STARVE, OR LEAP TO MY DEATH.
I GROPED MY WAY BACK TO THE WALL. STARVATION WAS PREFERABLE TO THAT PIT.

I HAD BEEN QUITE OFF IN MY ESTIMATE OF THE DUNGEON'S SIZE. IT WAS HALF AS LARGE AS I HAD GUESSED.

THEN THE TRUTH FLASHED UPON ME.

HOW COULD I HAVE BEEN SO MISTAKEN?

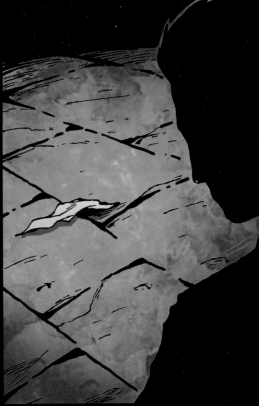

IN MY FIRST ATTEMPT AT CIRCLING THE ROOM, I HAD COUNTED FIFTY-TWO PACES BEFORE I PASSED OUT.

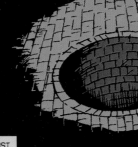

UPON AWAKENING, I MUST HAVE RETURNED IN THE WRONG DIRECTION AS I FOLLOWED THE WALLS.

BUT AS I LOOKED UP AT THE WALLS, I SAW SOMETHING TRULY SURPRISING--AND HORRIFYING.

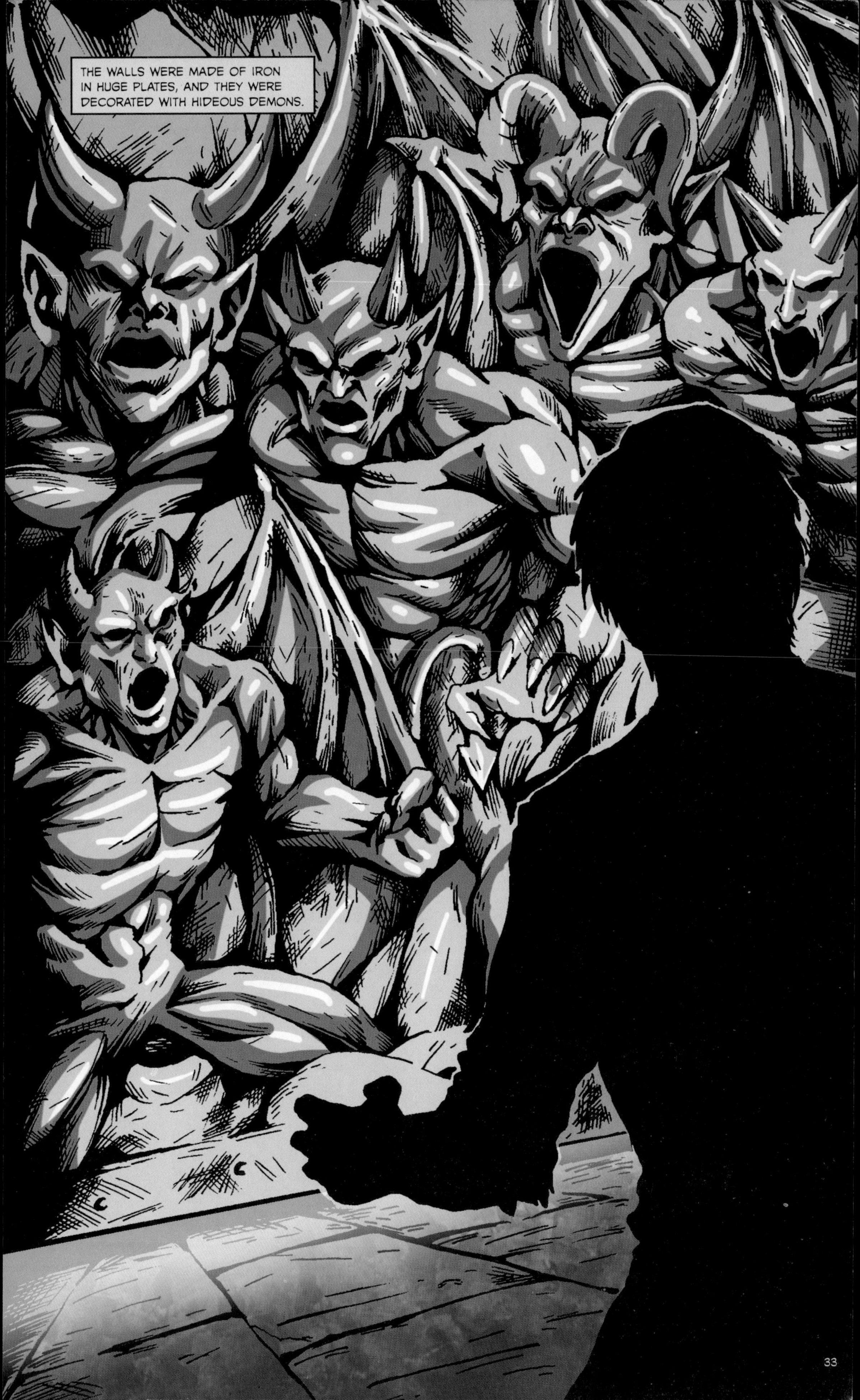
THE WALLS WERE MADE OF IRON IN HUGE PLATES, AND THEY WERE DECORATED WITH HIDEOUS DEMONS.

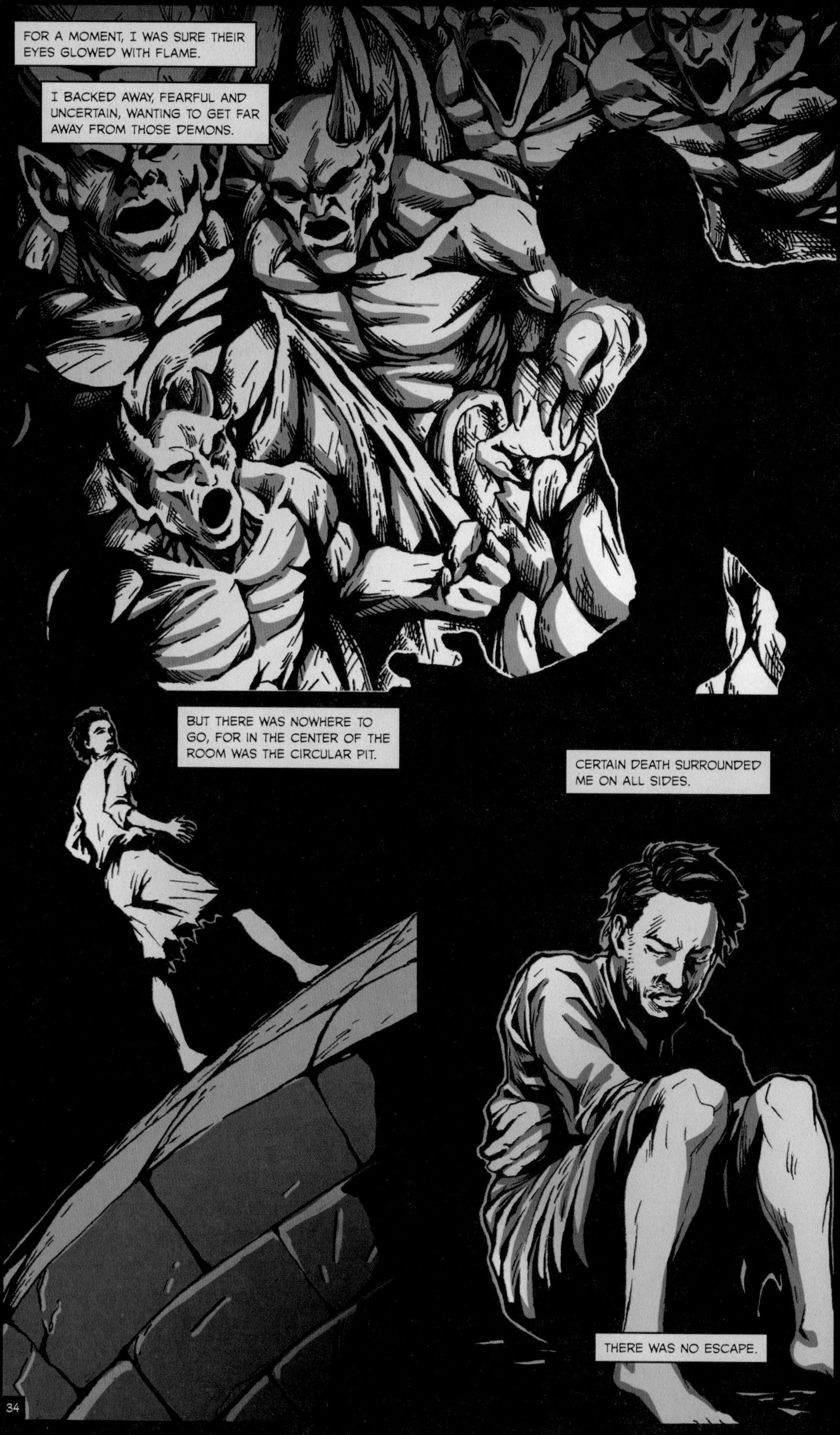
FOR A MOMENT, I WAS SURE THEIR EYES GLOWED WITH FLAME.
I BACKED AWAY, FEARFUL AND UNCERTAIN, WANTING TO GET FAR AWAY FROM THOSE DEMONS.
BUT THERE WAS NOWHERE TO GO, FOR IN THE CENTER OF THE ROOM WAS THE CIRCULAR PIT.
CERTAIN DEATH SURROUNDED ME ON ALL SIDES.
THERE WAS NO ESCAPE.

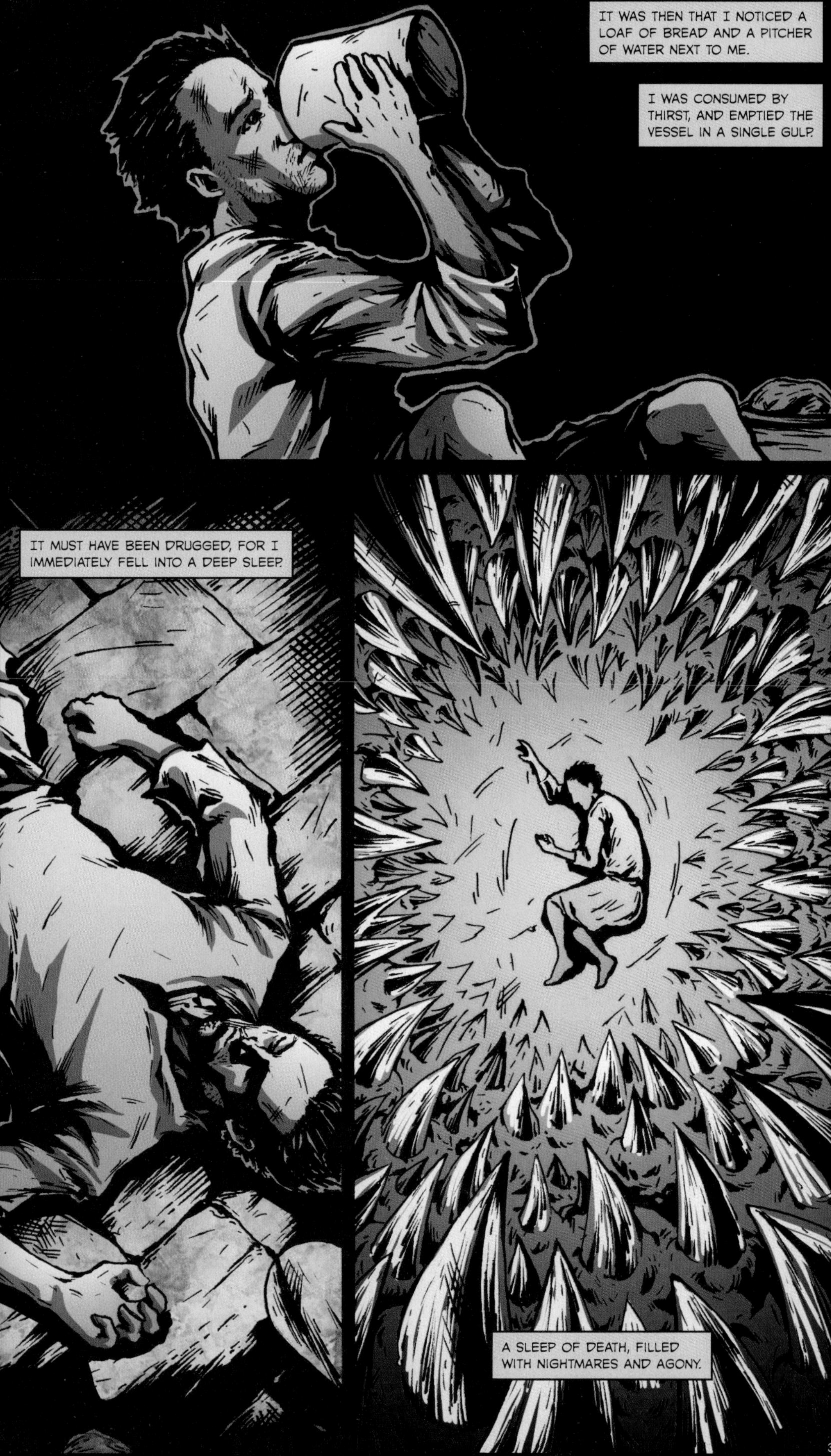
IT WAS THEN THAT I NOTICED A LOAF OF BREAD AND A PITCHER OF WATER NEXT TO ME.
I WAS CONSUMED BY THIRST, AND EMPTIED THE VESSEL IN A SINGLE GULP.
IT MUST HAVE BEEN DRUGGED, FOR I IMMEDIATELY FELL INTO A DEEP SLEEP.
A SLEEP OF DEATH, FILLED WITH NIGHTMARES AND AGONY.

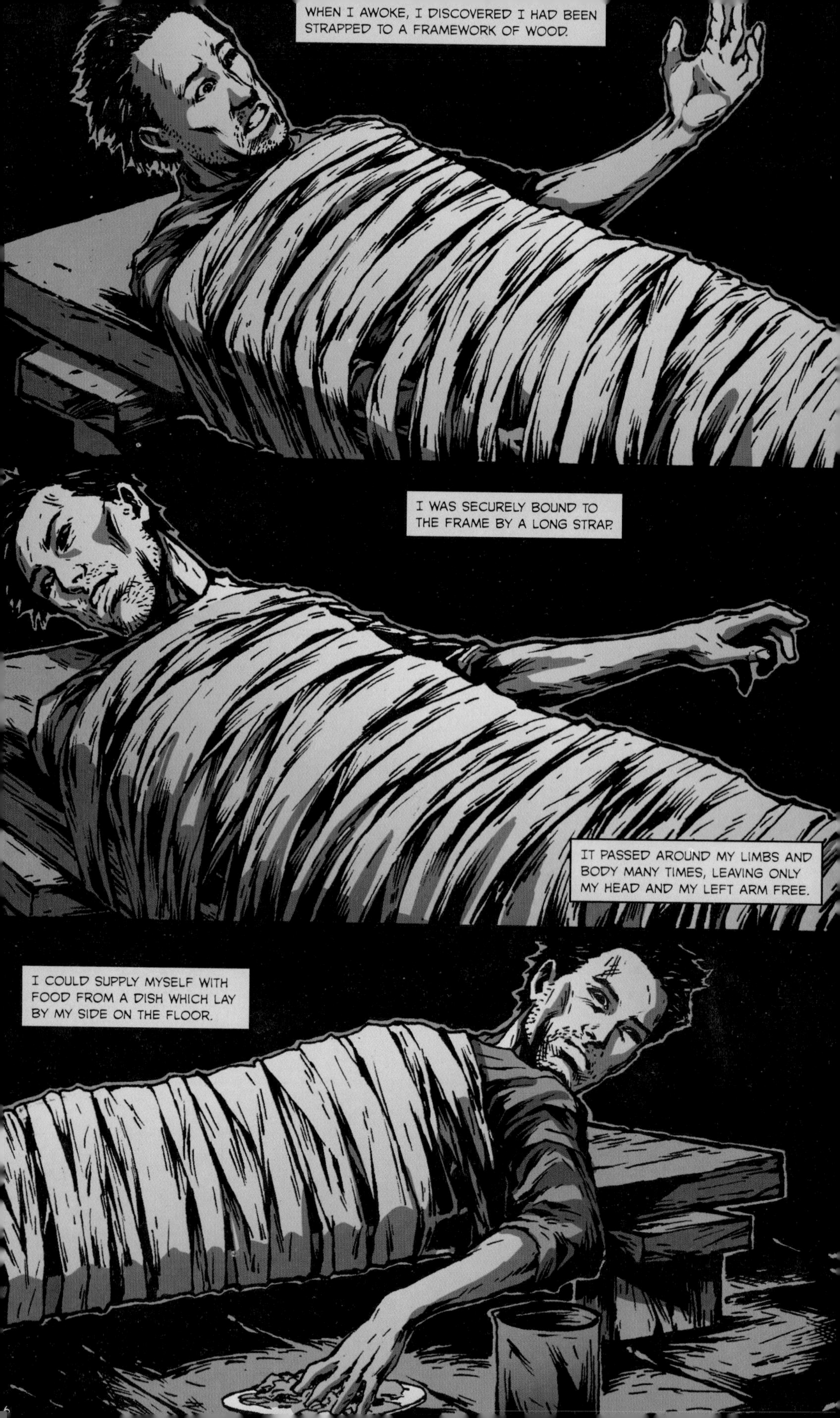
WHEN I AWOKE, I DISCOVERED I HAD BEEN STRAPPED TO A FRAMEWORK OF WOOD.
I WAS SECURELY BOUND TO THE FRAME BY A LONG STRAP.
IT PASSED AROUND MY LIMBS AND BODY MANY TIMES, LEAVING ONLY MY HEAD AND MY LEFT ARM FREE.
I COULD SUPPLY MYSELF WITH FOOD FROM A DISH WHICH LAY BY MY SIDE ON THE FLOOR.

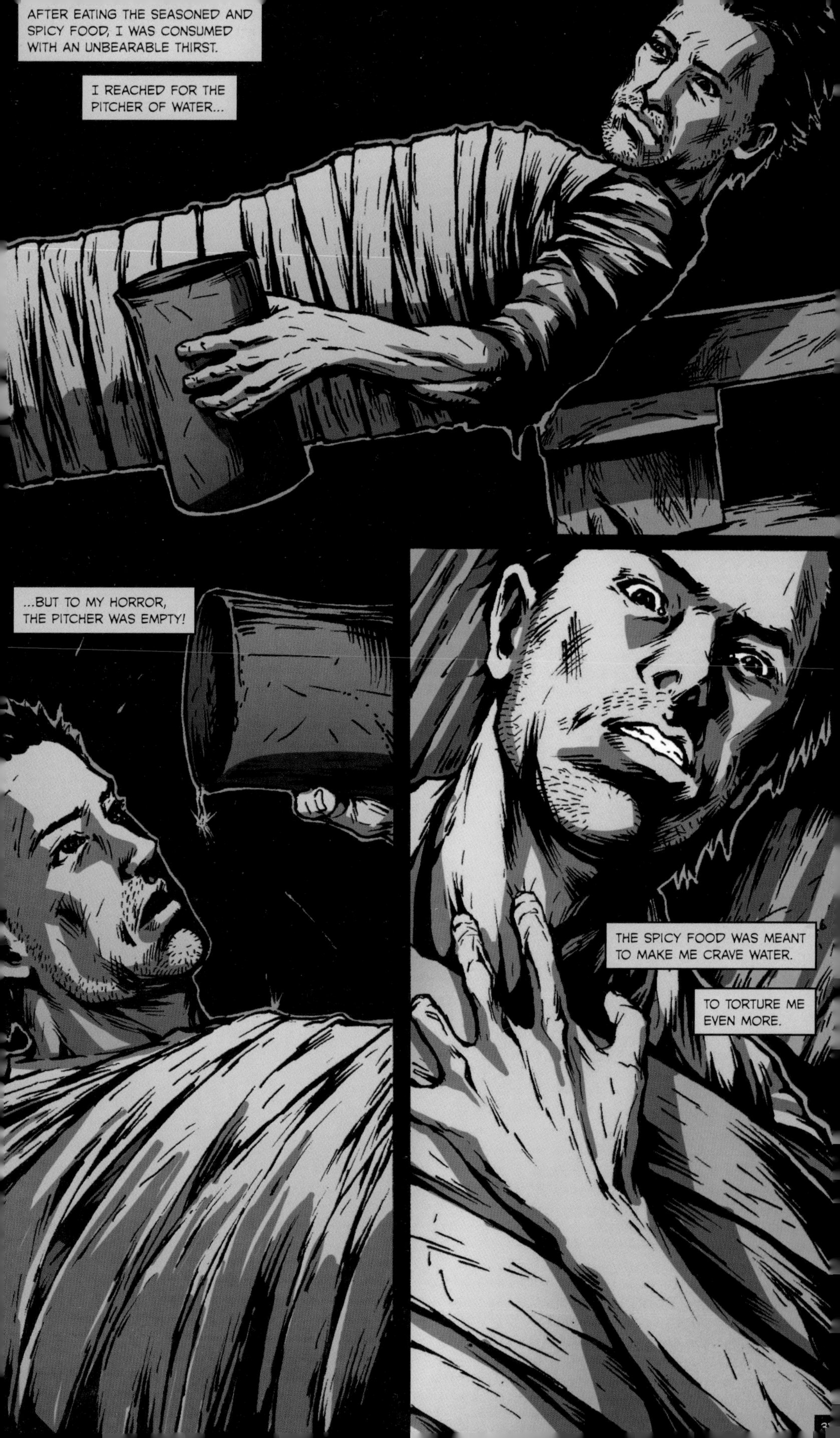
AFTER EATING THE SEASONED AND SPICY FOOD, I WAS CONSUMED WITH AN UNBEARABLE THIRST.
I REACHED FOR THE PITCHER OF WATER...
...BUT TO MY HORROR, THE PITCHER WAS EMPTY!
THE SPICY FOOD WAS MEANT TO MAKE ME CRAVE WATER.
TO TORTURE ME EVEN MORE.

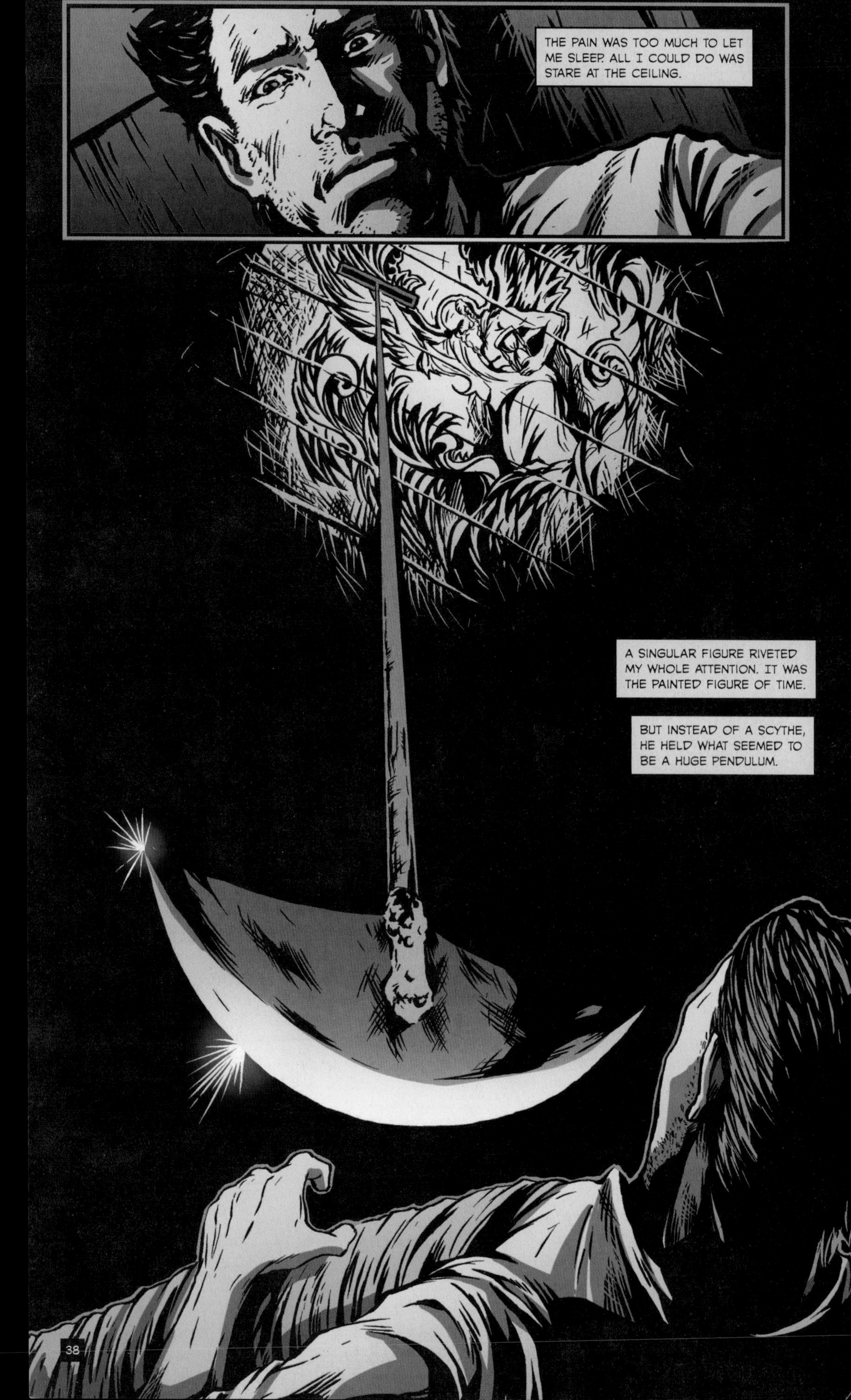
THE PAIN WAS TOO MUCH TO LET ME SLEEP. ALL I COULD DO WAS STARE AT THE CEILING.
A SINGULAR FIGURE RIVETED MY WHOLE ATTENTION. IT WAS THE PAINTED FIGURE OF TIME.
BUT INSTEAD OF A SCYTHE, HE HELD WHAT SEEMED TO BE A HUGE PENDULUM.

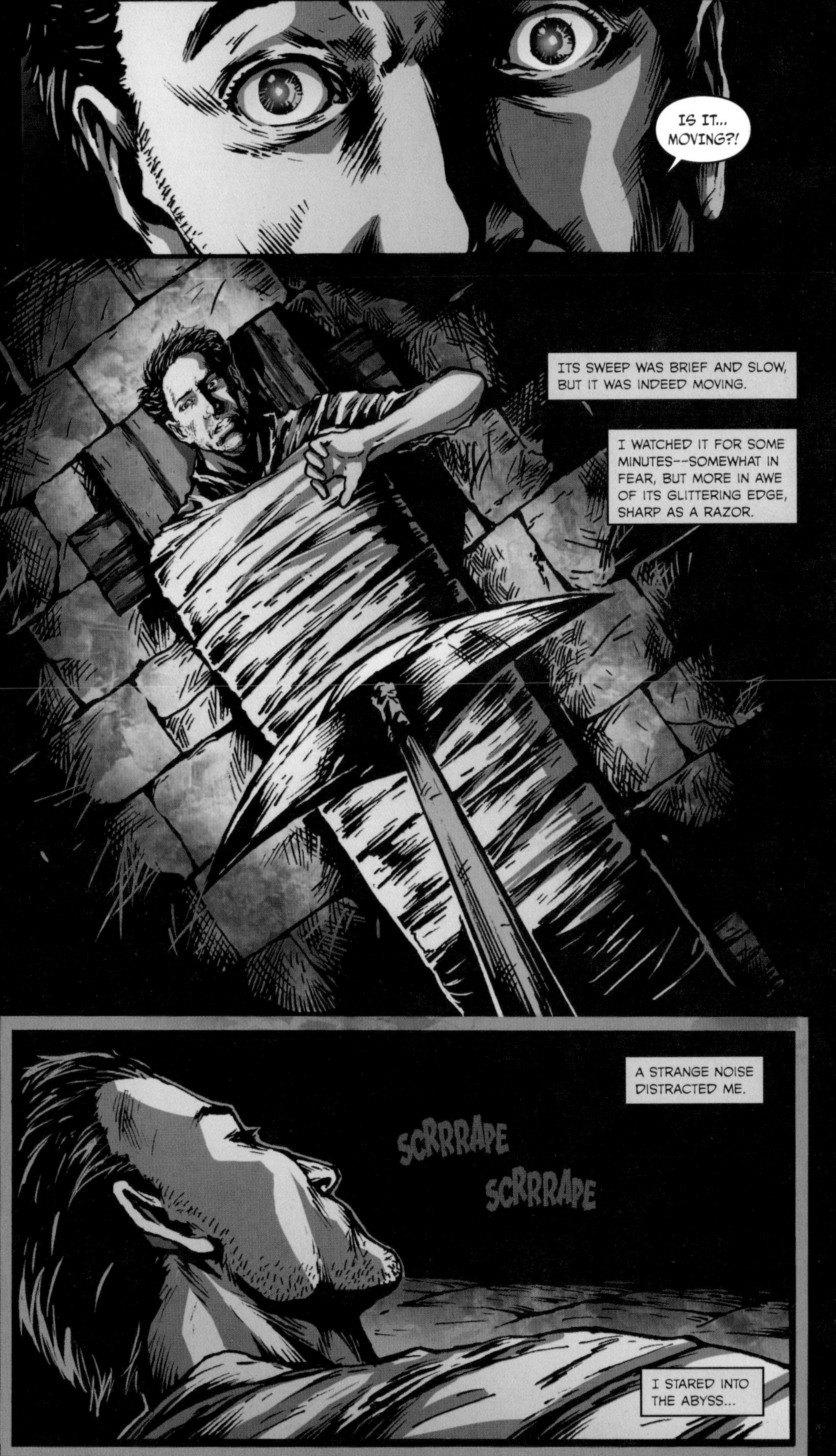
IS IT... MOVING?!
ITS SWEEP WAS BRIEF AND SLOW, BUT IT WAS INDEED MOVING.
I WATCHED IT FOR SOME MINUTES--SOMEWHAT IN FEAR, BUT MORE IN AWE OF ITS GLITTERING EDGE, SHARP AS A RAZOR.
A STRANGE NOISE DISTRACTED ME.
SCRRRAPE
SCRRRAPE
I STARED INTO THE ABYSS...

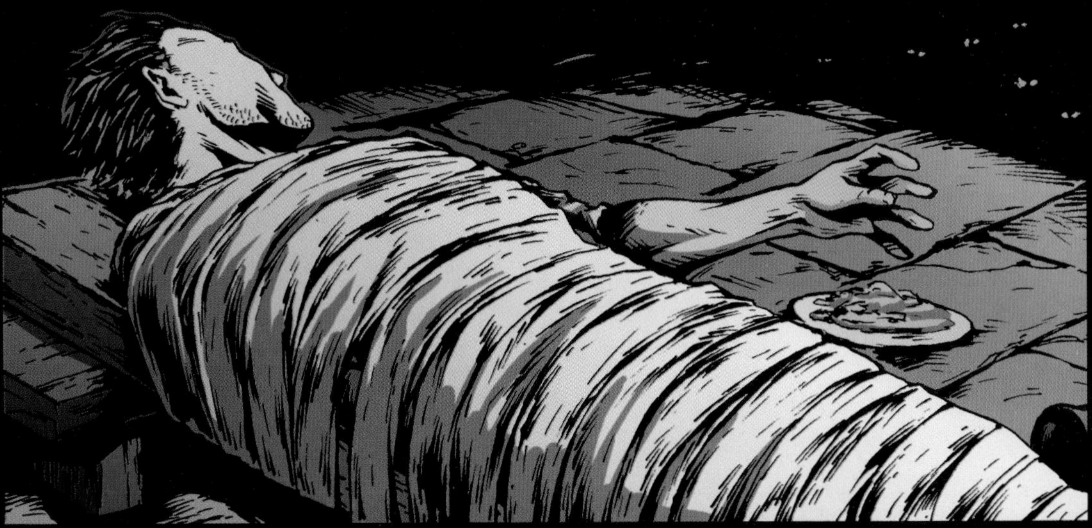
...AND SAW SOMETHING STARING BACK AT ME.

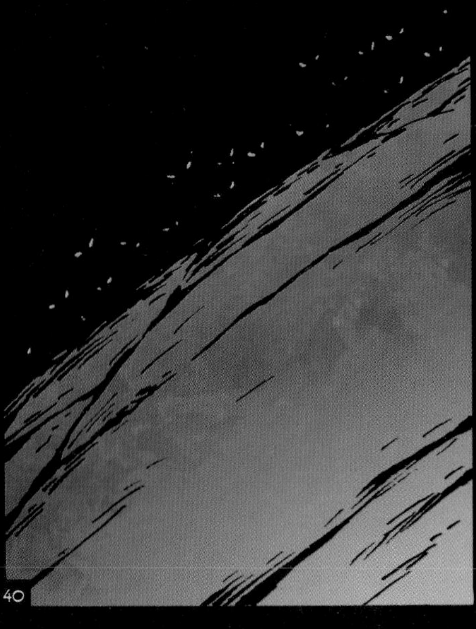
SEVERAL SOMETHINGS.

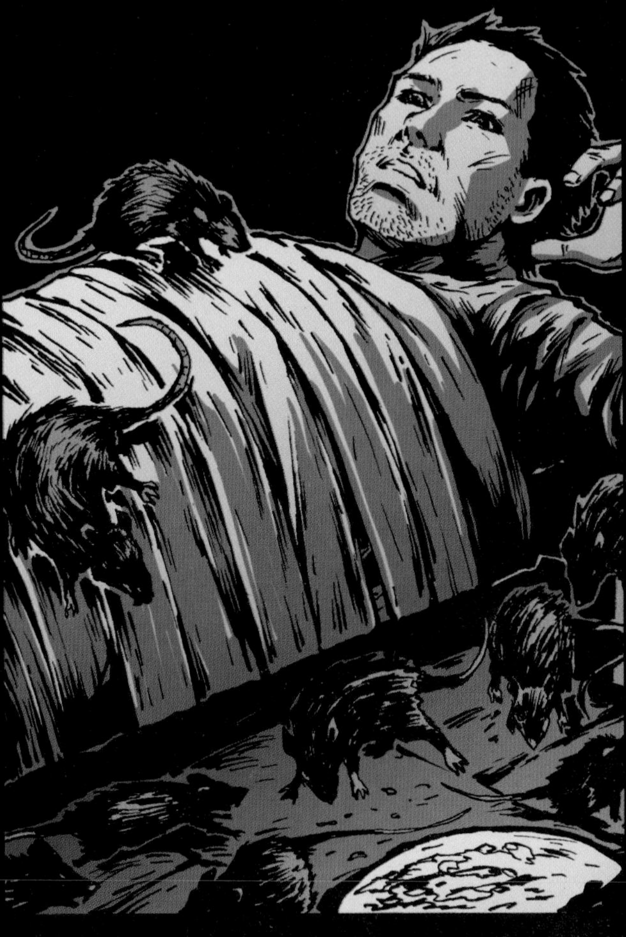
THEY CAME UP HURRIEDLY TOWARD THE SCENT OF THE MEAT.

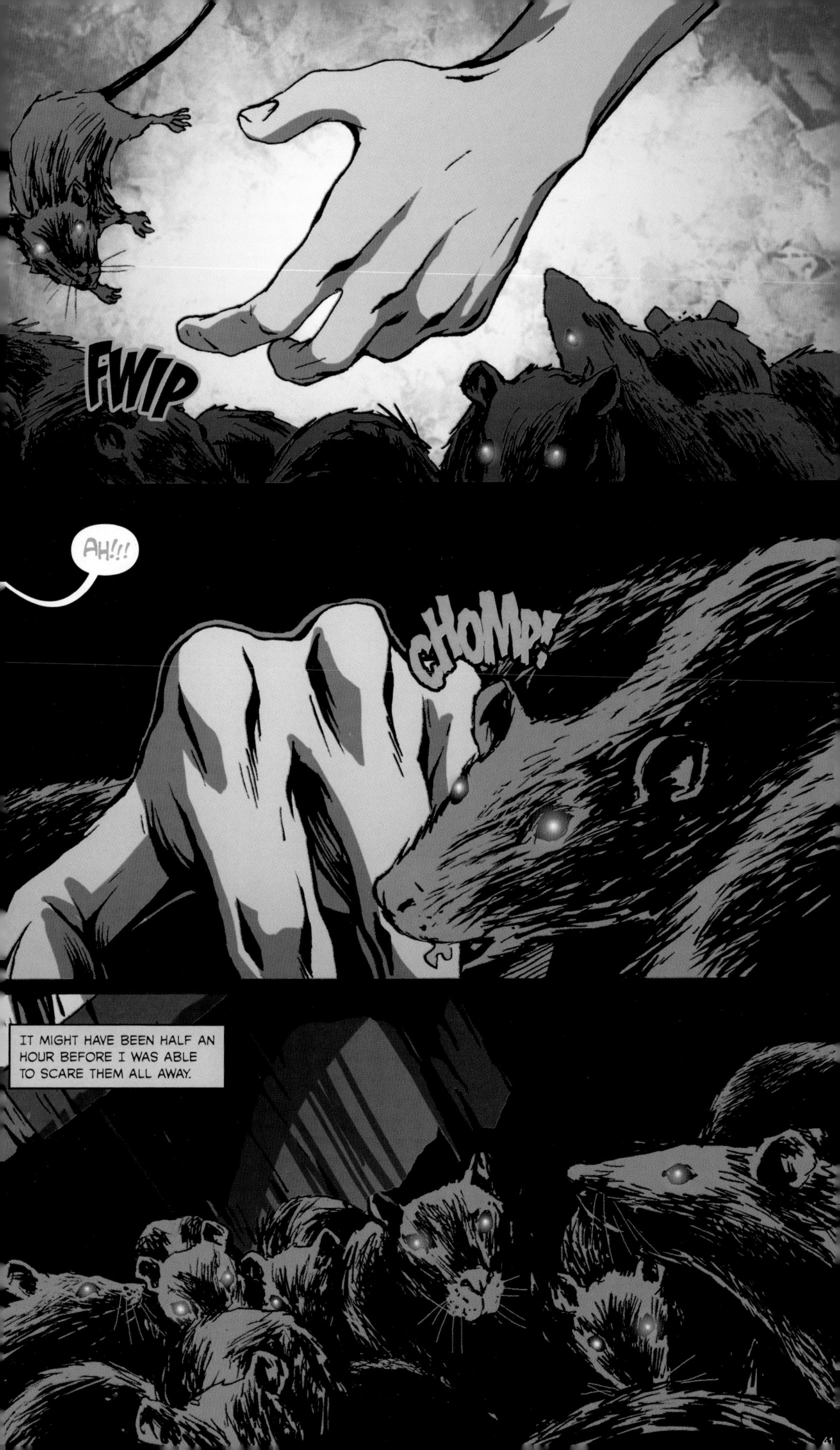
FWIP
AH!!!
CHOMP!
IT MIGHT HAVE BEEN HALF AN HOUR BEFORE I WAS ABLE TO SCARE THEM ALL AWAY.

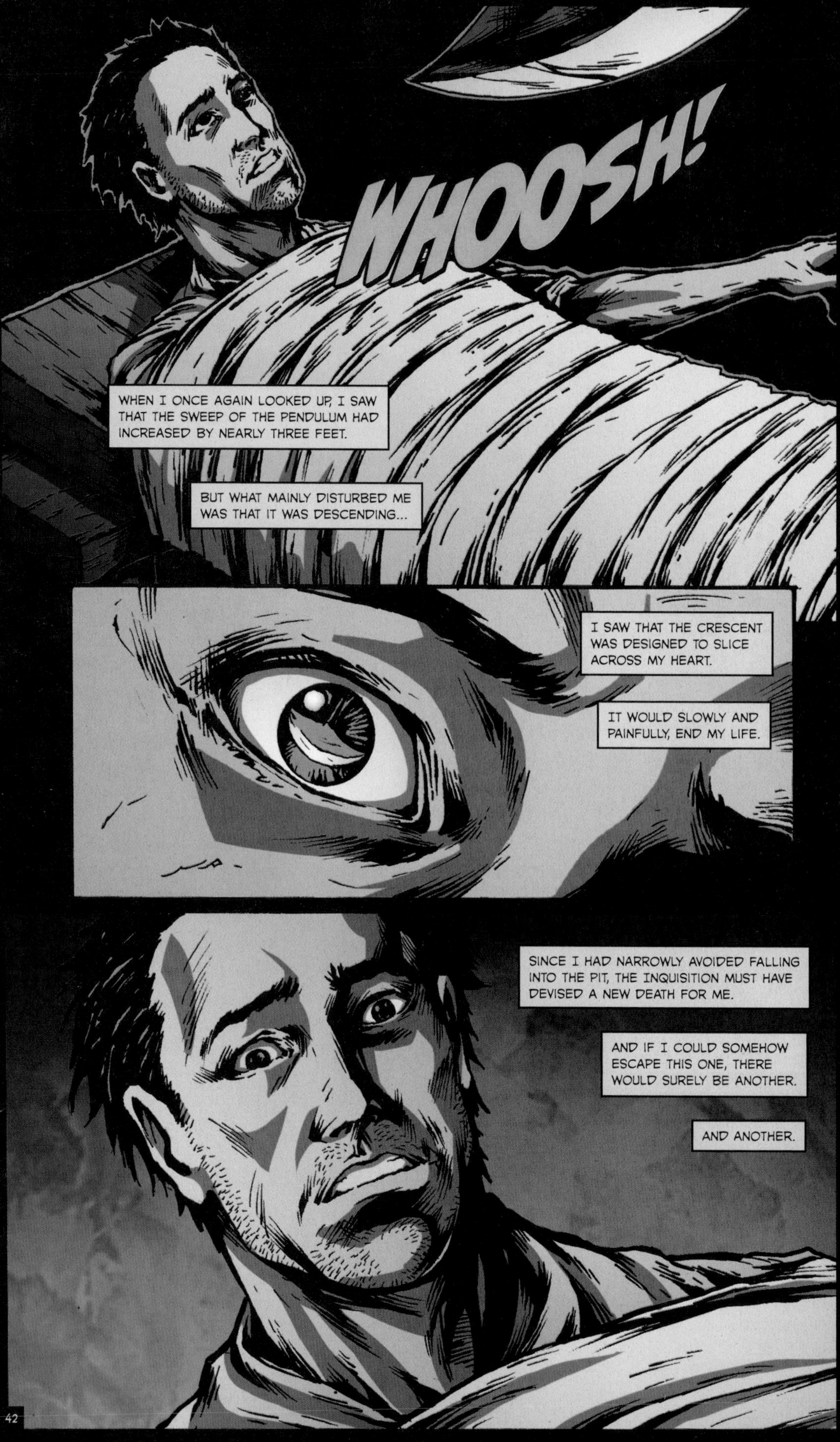
WHOOSH!
WHEN I ONCE AGAIN LOOKED UP, I SAW THAT THE SWEEP OF THE PENDULUM HAD INCREASED BY NEARLY THREE FEET.
BUT WHAT MAINLY DISTURBED ME WAS THAT IT WAS DESCENDING...
I SAW THAT THE CRESCENT WAS DESIGNED TO SLICE ACROSS MY HEART.
IT WOULD SLOWLY AND PAINFULLY, END MY LIFE.
SINCE I HAD NARROWLY AVOIDED FALLING INTO THE PIT, THE INQUISITION MUST HAVE DEVISED A NEW DEATH FOR ME.
AND IF I COULD SOMEHOW ESCAPE THIS ONE, THERE WOULD SURELY BE ANOTHER.
AND ANOTHER.

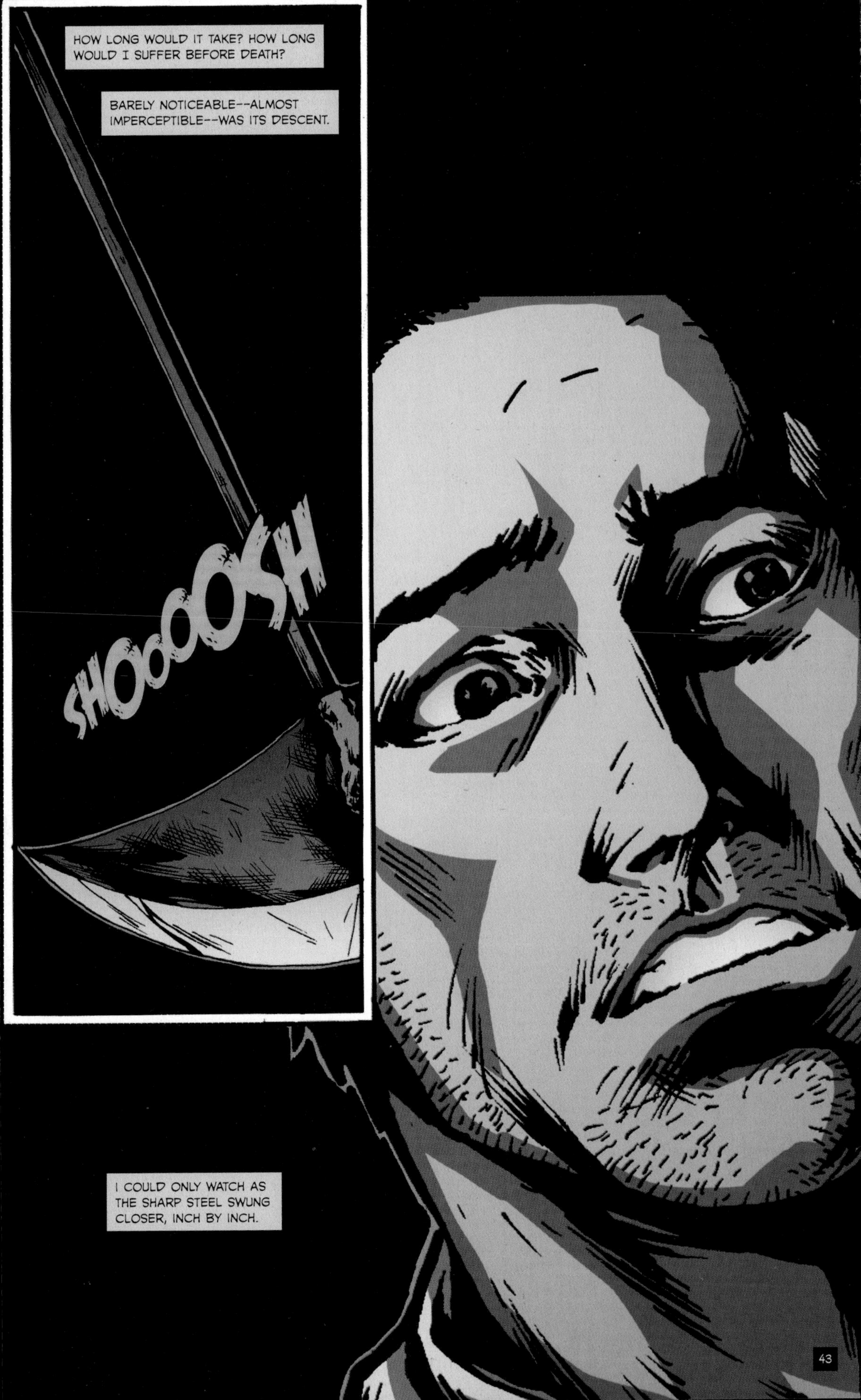
HOW LONG WOULD IT TAKE? HOW LONG WOULD I SUFFER BEFORE DEATH?
BARELY NOTICEABLE--ALMOST IMPERCEPTIBLE--WAS ITS DESCENT.
SHOOOOSH
I COULD ONLY WATCH AS THE SHARP STEEL SWUNG CLOSER, INCH BY INCH.

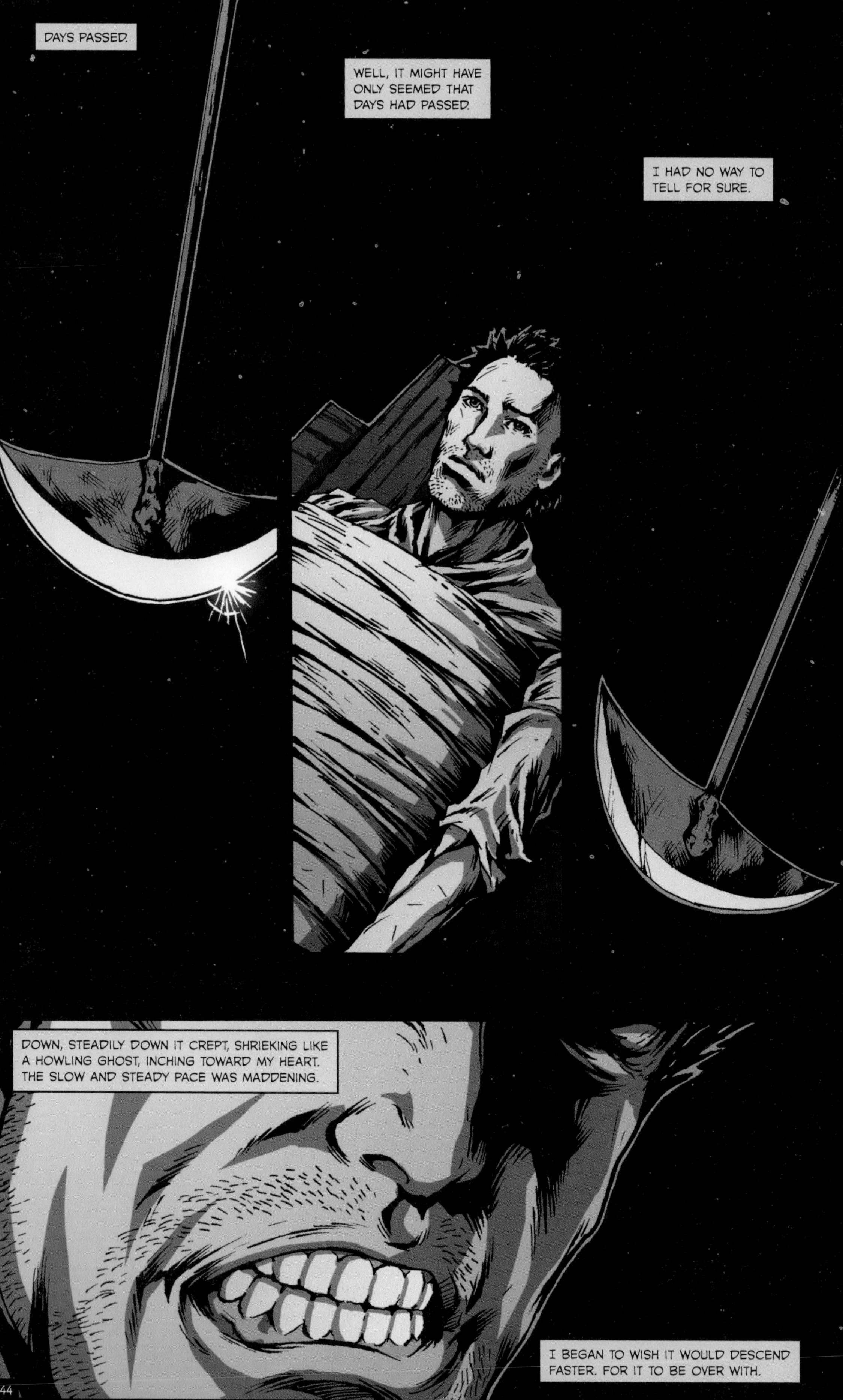
DAYS PASSED.
WELL, IT MIGHT HAVE ONLY SEEMED THAT DAYS HAD PASSED.
I HAD NO WAY TO TELL FOR SURE.
DOWN, STEADILY DOWN IT CREPT, SHRIEKING LIKE A HOWLING GHOST, INCHING TOWARD MY HEART. THE SLOW AND STEADY PACE WAS MADDENING.
I BEGAN TO WISH IT WOULD DESCEND FASTER. FOR IT TO BE OVER WITH.

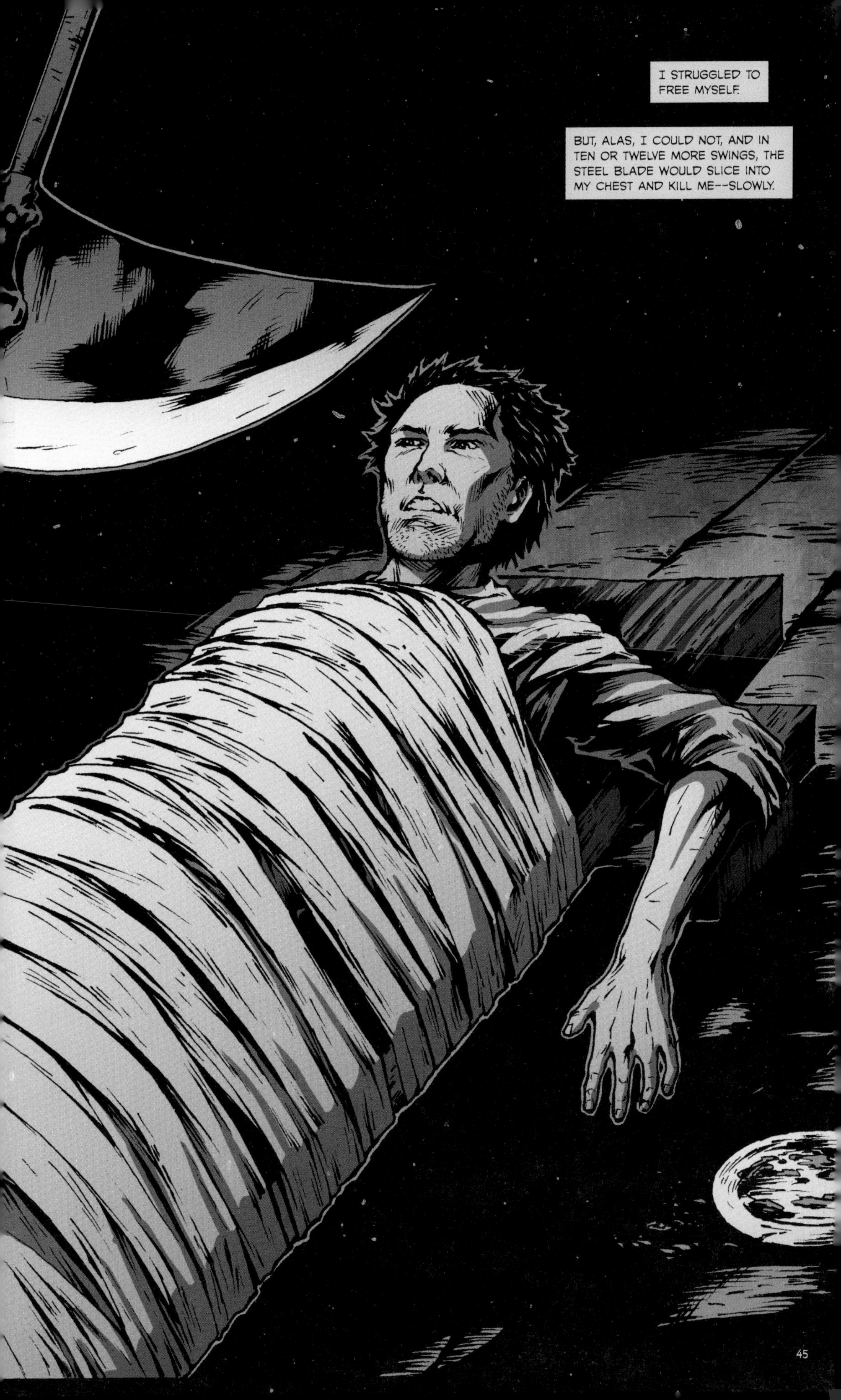
I STRUGGLED TO FREE MYSELF.
BUT, ALAS, I COULD NOT, AND IN TEN OR TWELVE MORE SWINGS, THE STEEL BLADE WOULD SLICE INTO MY CHEST AND KILL ME--SLOWLY.

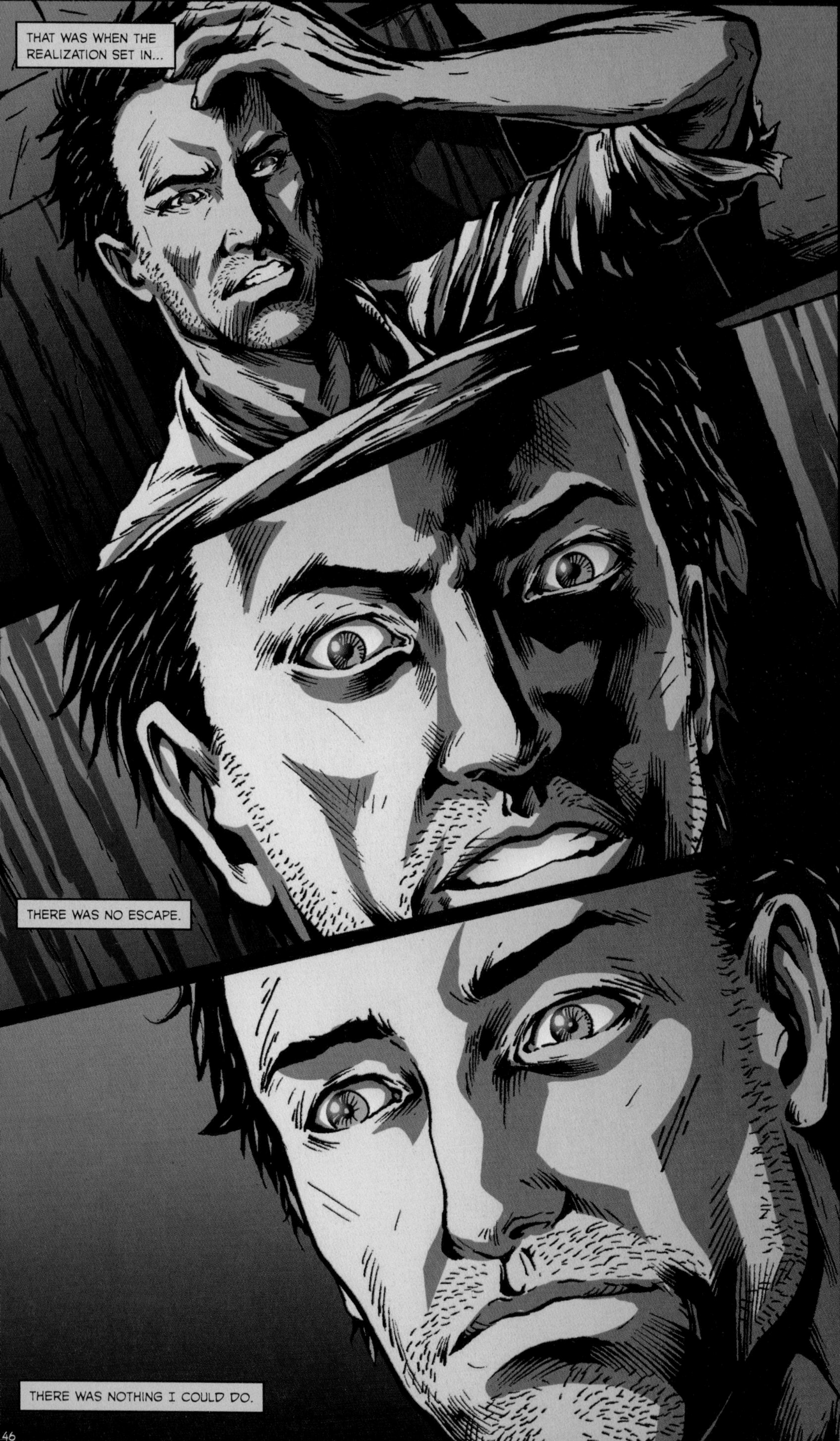
THAT WAS WHEN THE REALIZATION SET IN...
THERE WAS NO ESCAPE.
THERE WAS NOTHING I COULD DO.

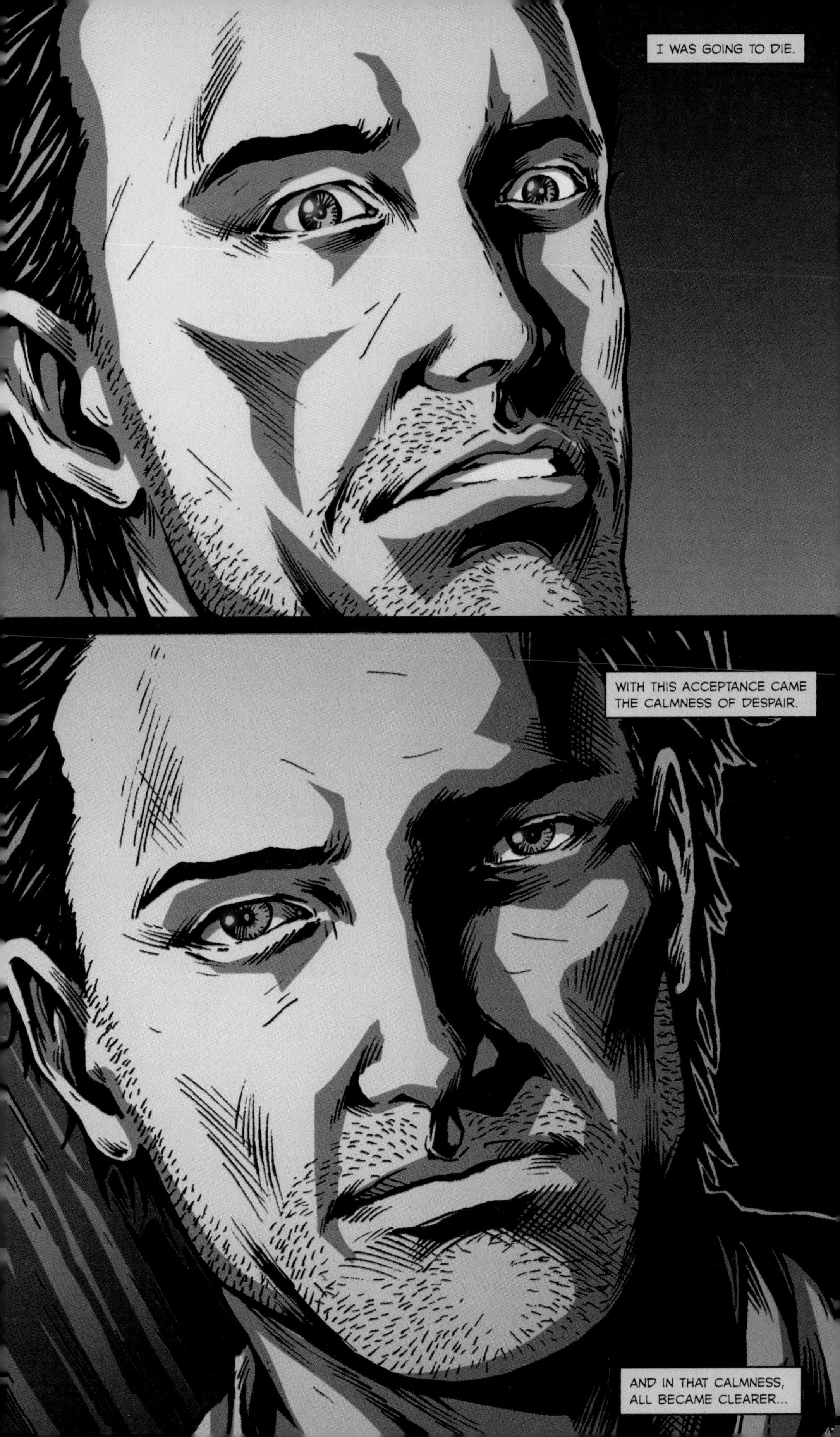
I WAS GOING TO DIE.
WITH THIS ACCEPTANCE CAME THE CALMNESS OF DESPAIR.
AND IN THAT CALMNESS, ALL BECAME CLEARER...

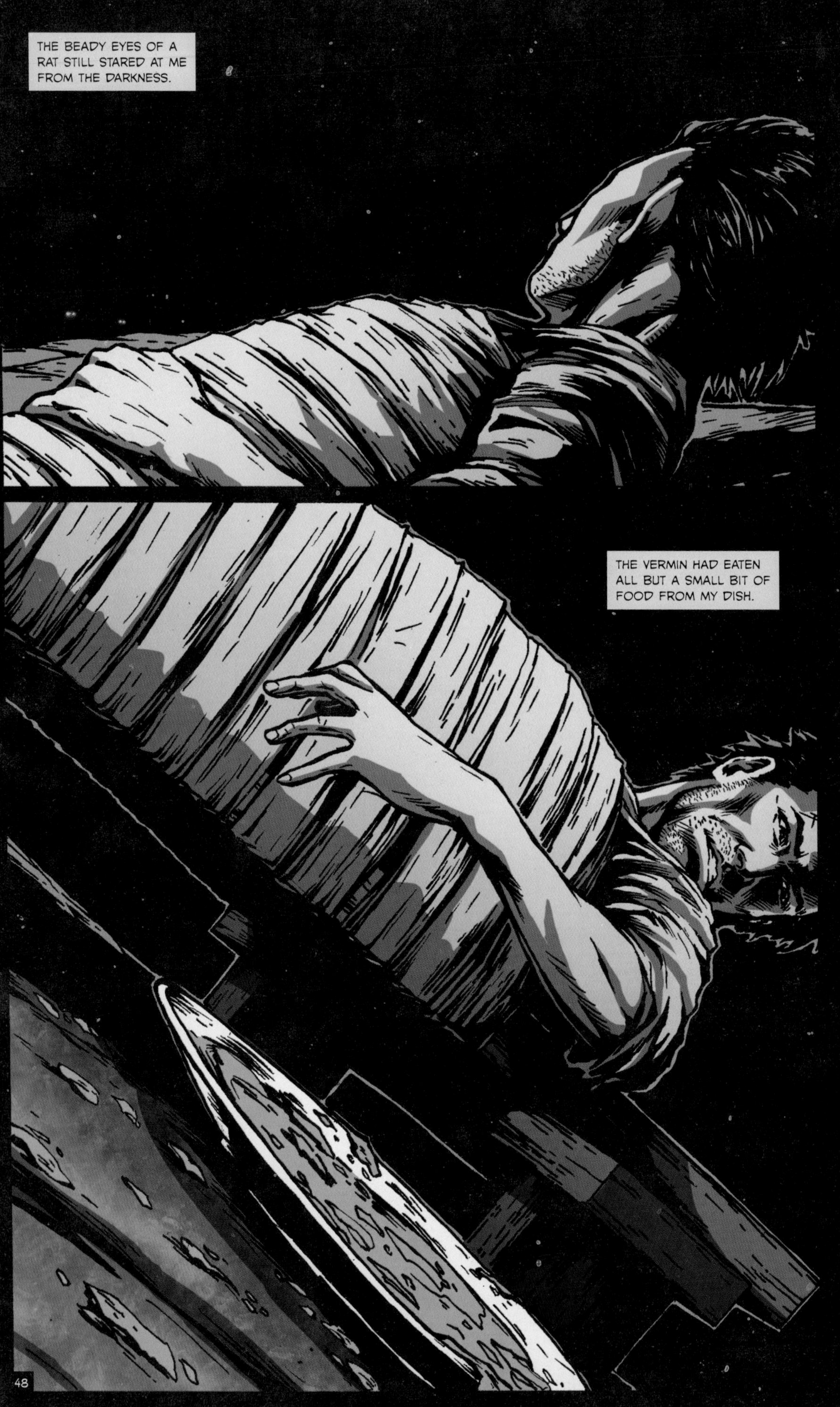
THE BEADY EYES OF A RAT STILL STARED AT ME FROM THE DARKNESS.
THE VERMIN HAD EATEN ALL BUT A SMALL BIT OF FOOD FROM MY DISH.

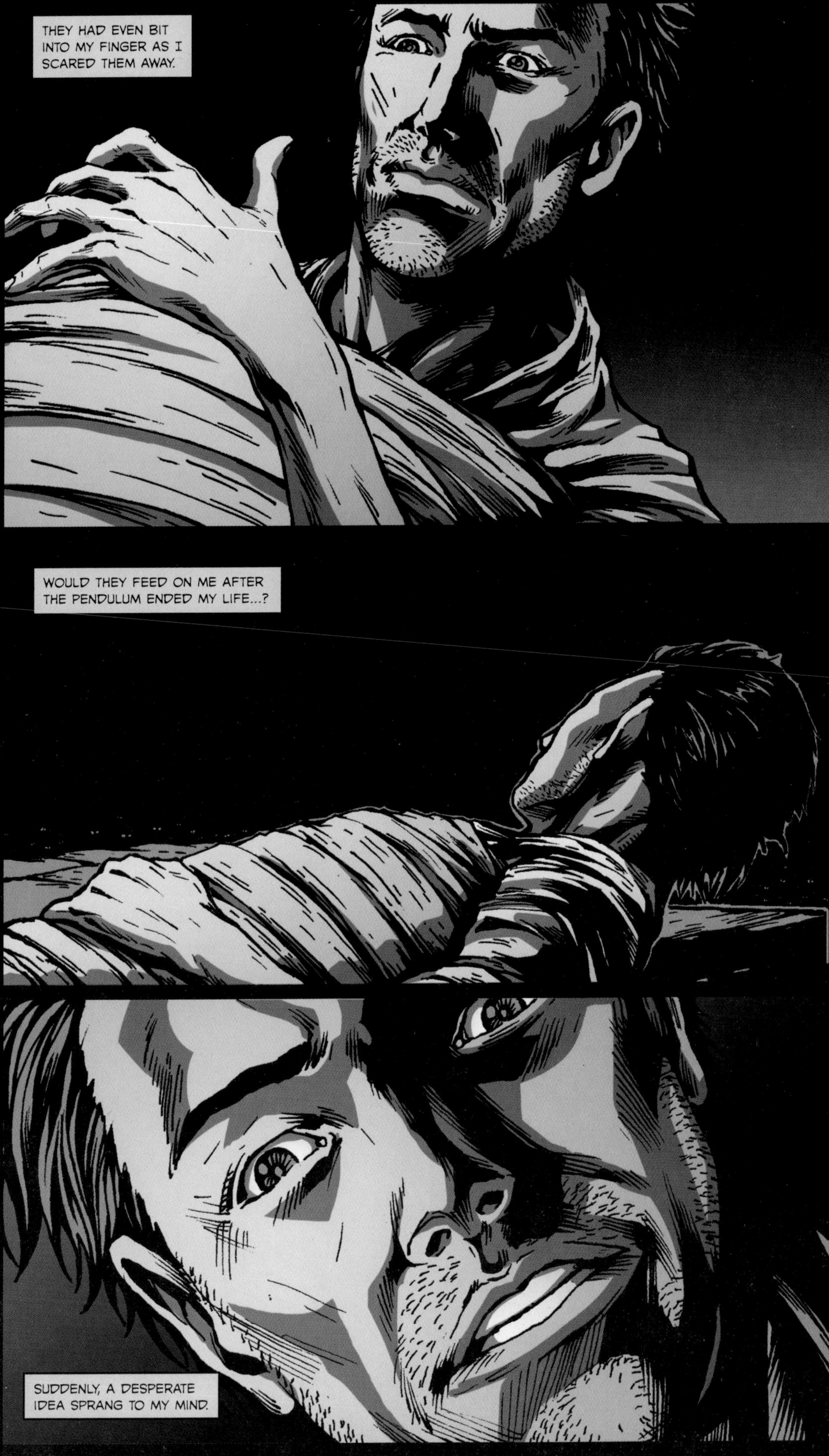
THEY HAD EVEN BIT INTO MY FINGER AS I SCARED THEM AWAY.
WOULD THEY FEED ON ME AFTER THE PENDULUM ENDED MY LIFE...?
SUDDENLY, A DESPERATE IDEA SPRANG TO MY MIND.

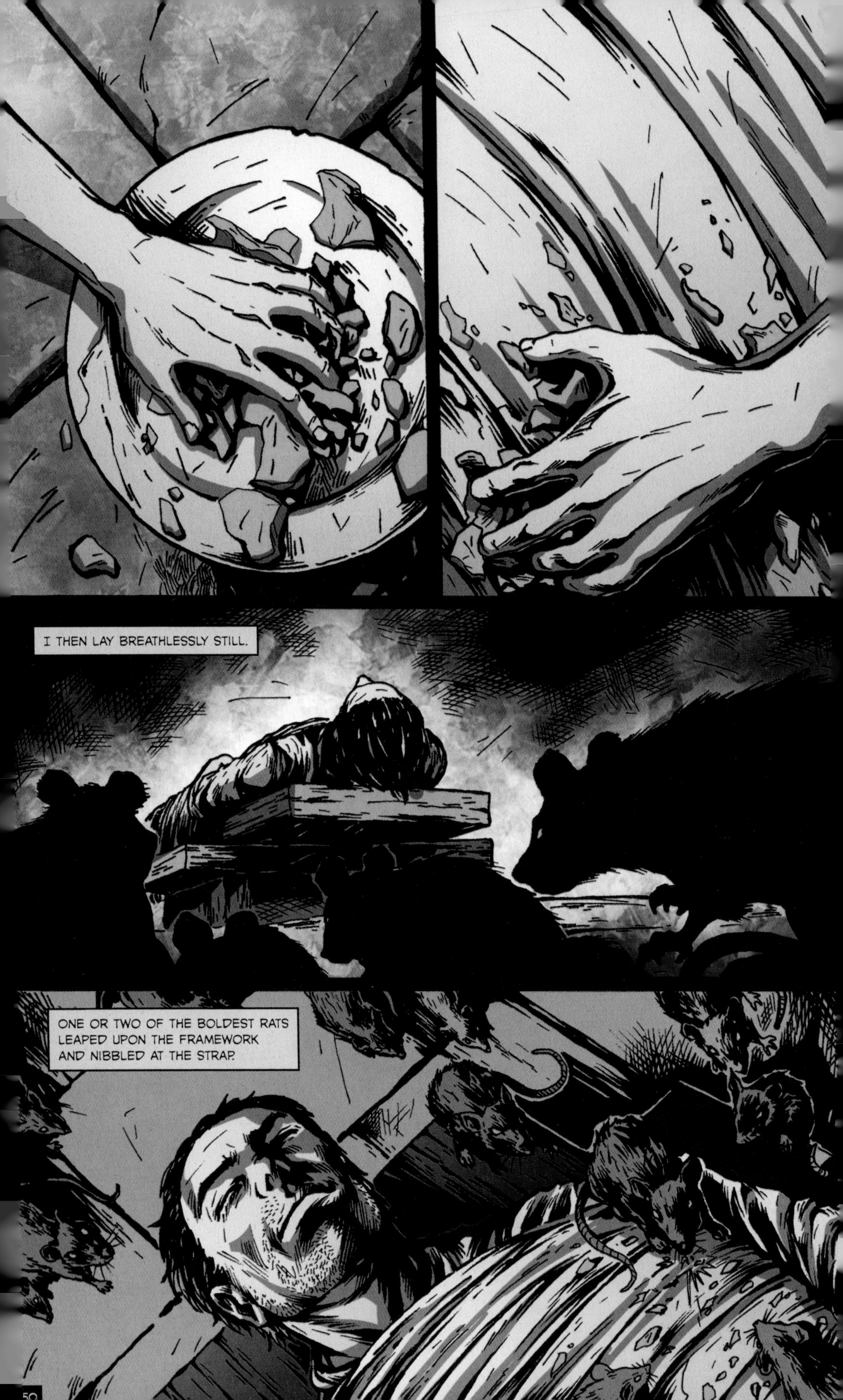

I THEN LAY BREATHLESSLY STILL.
ONE OR TWO OF THE BOLDEST RATS LEAPED UPON THE FRAMEWORK AND NIBBLED AT THE STRAP.

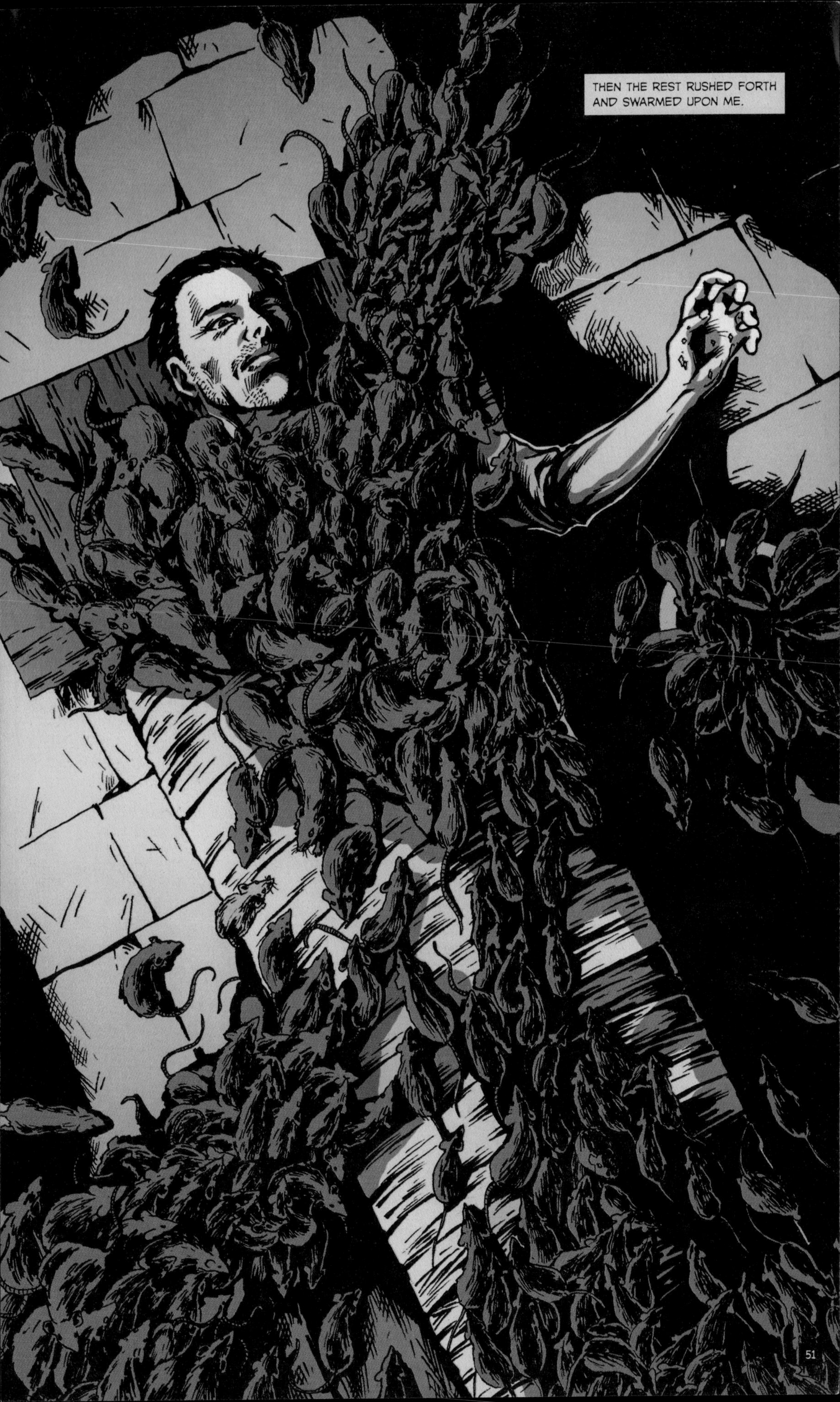
THEN THE REST RUSHED FORTH
AND SWARMED UPON ME.

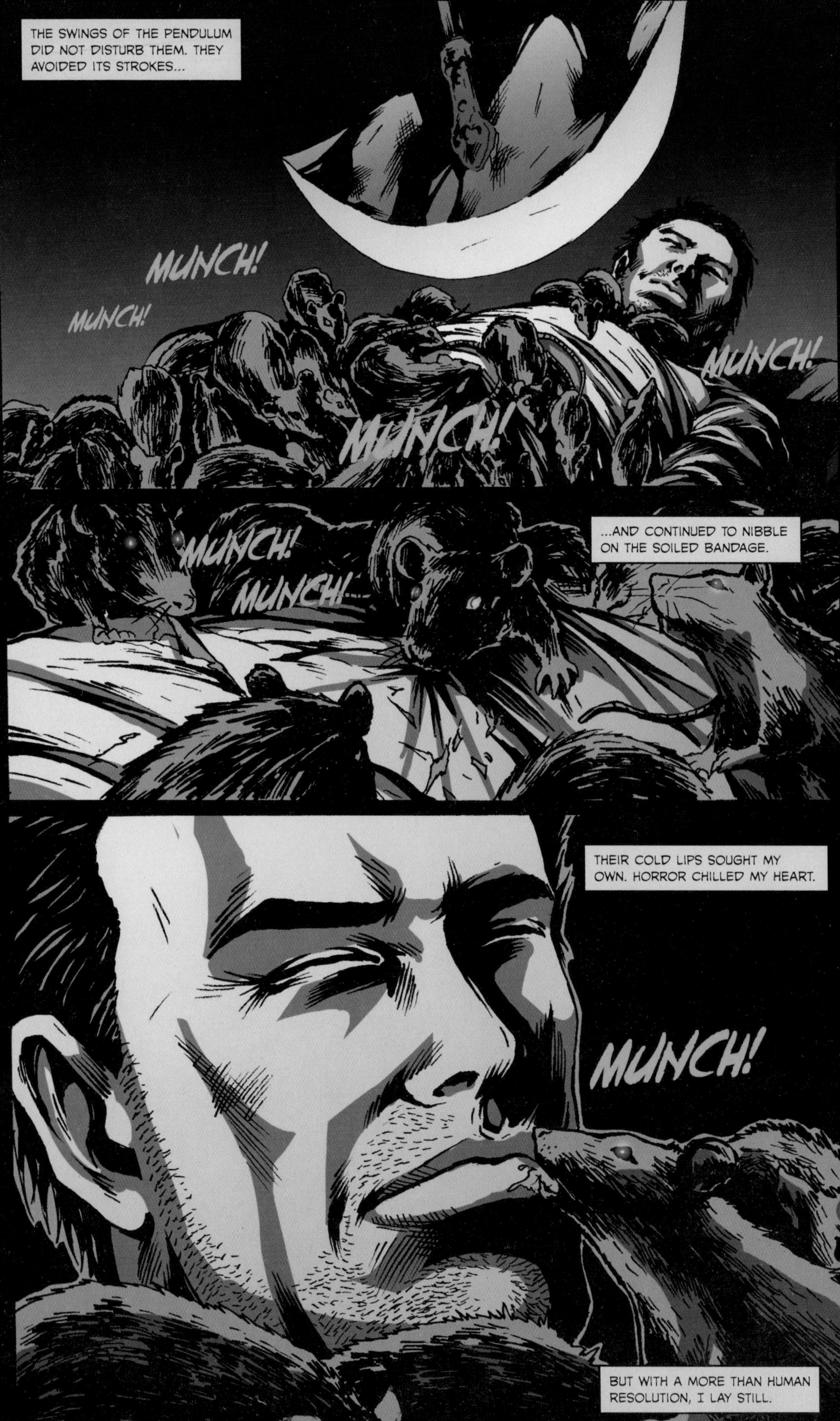
THE SWINGS OF THE PENDULUM DID NOT DISTURB THEM. THEY AVOIDED ITS STROKES...
MUNCH!
MUNCH!
MUNCH!
MUNCH!
...AND CONTINUED TO NIBBLE ON THE SOILED BANDAGE.
MUNCH!
MUNCH!
THEIR COLD LIPS SOUGHT MY OWN. HORROR CHILLED MY HEART.
MUNCH!
BUT WITH A MORE THAN HUMAN RESOLUTION, I LAY STILL.

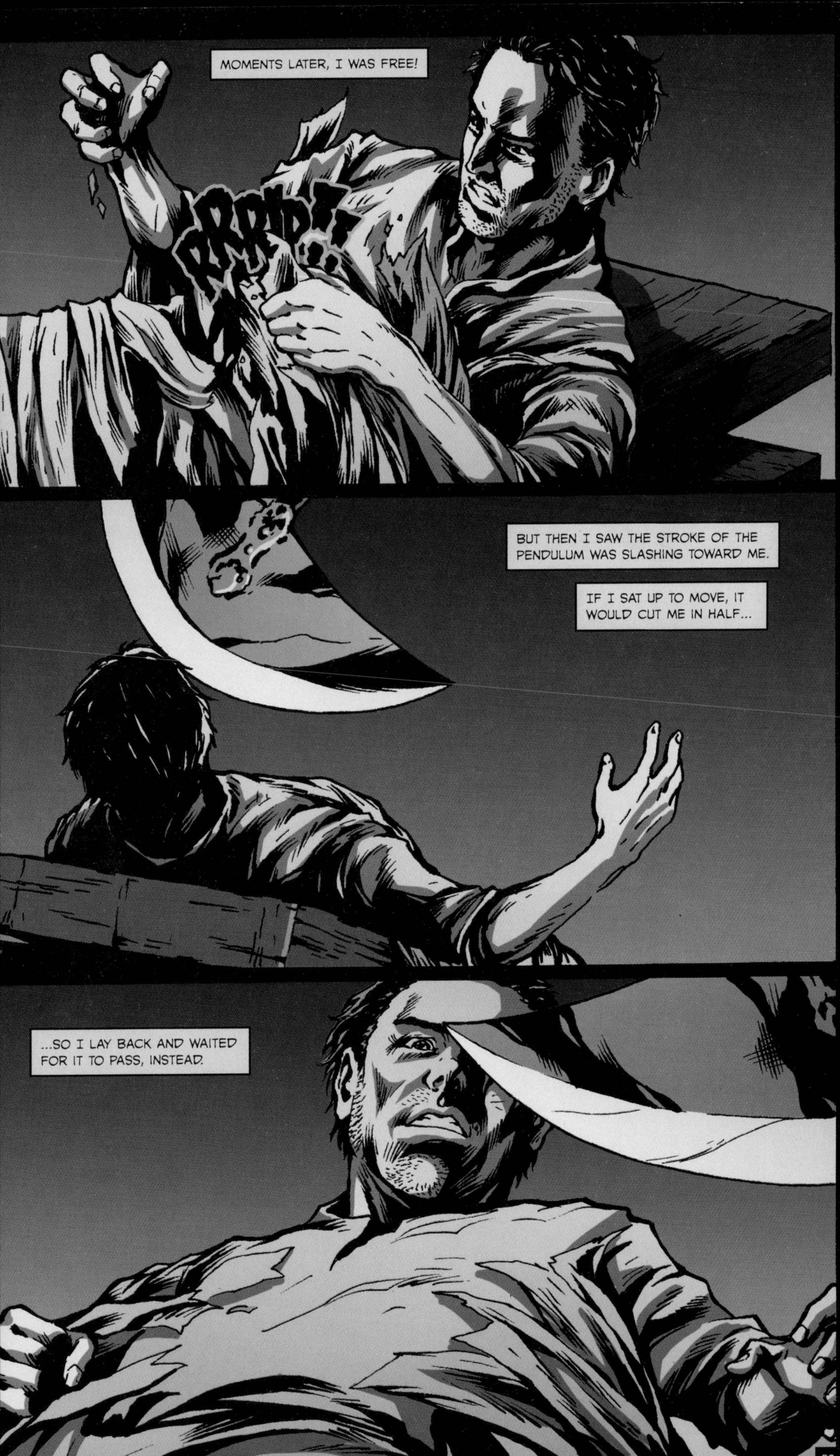
MOMENTS LATER, I WAS FREE!
BUT THEN I SAW THE STROKE OF THE PENDULUM WAS SLASHING TOWARD ME.
IF I SAT UP TO MOVE, IT WOULD CUT ME IN HALF...
...SO I LAY BACK AND WAITED FOR IT TO PASS, INSTEAD.

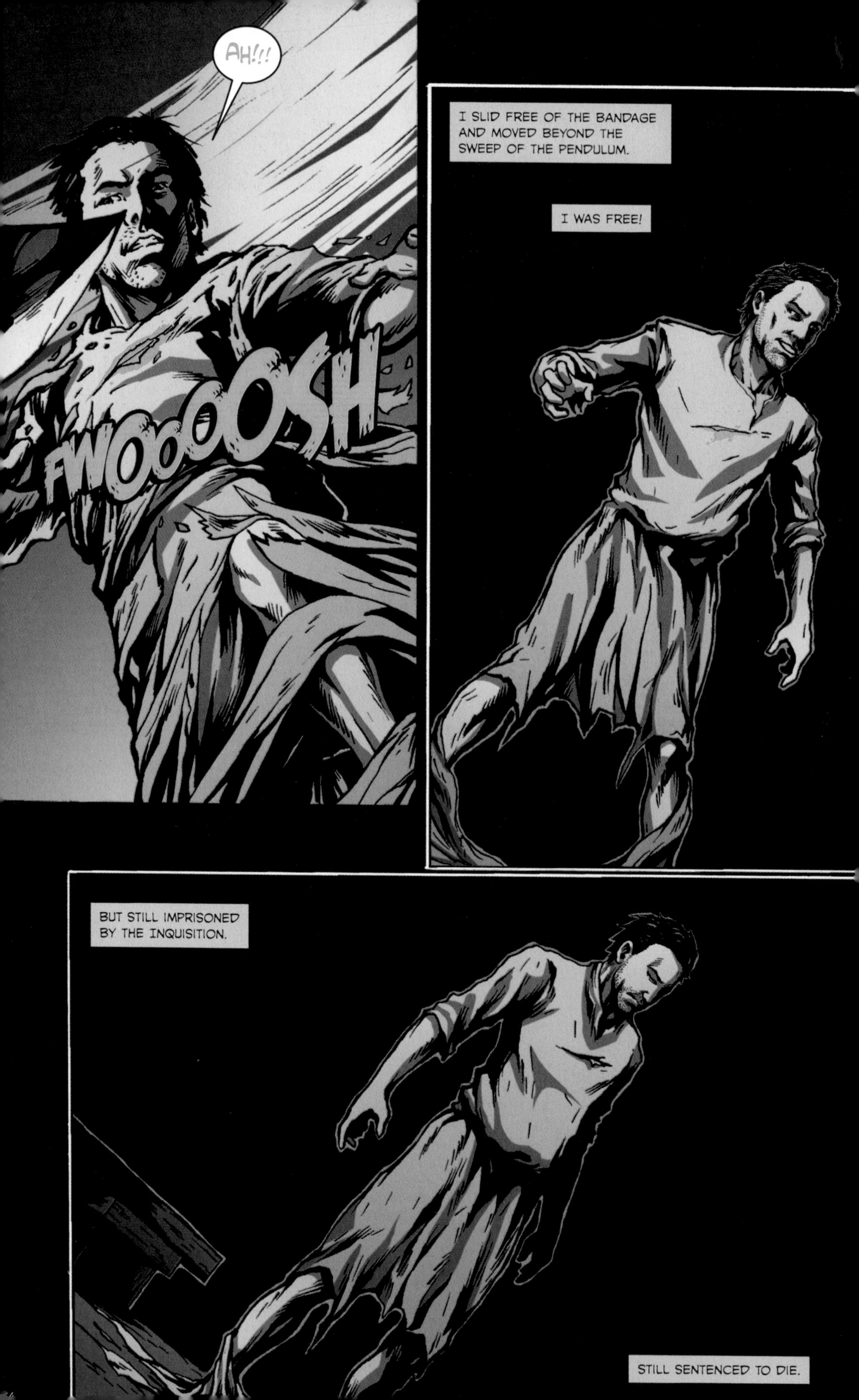
AH!!!
FWOOOOOSH
I SLID FREE OF THE BANDAGE AND MOVED BEYOND THE SWEEP OF THE PENDULUM.
I WAS FREE!
BUT STILL IMPRISONED BY THE INQUISITION.
STILL SENTENCED TO DIE.

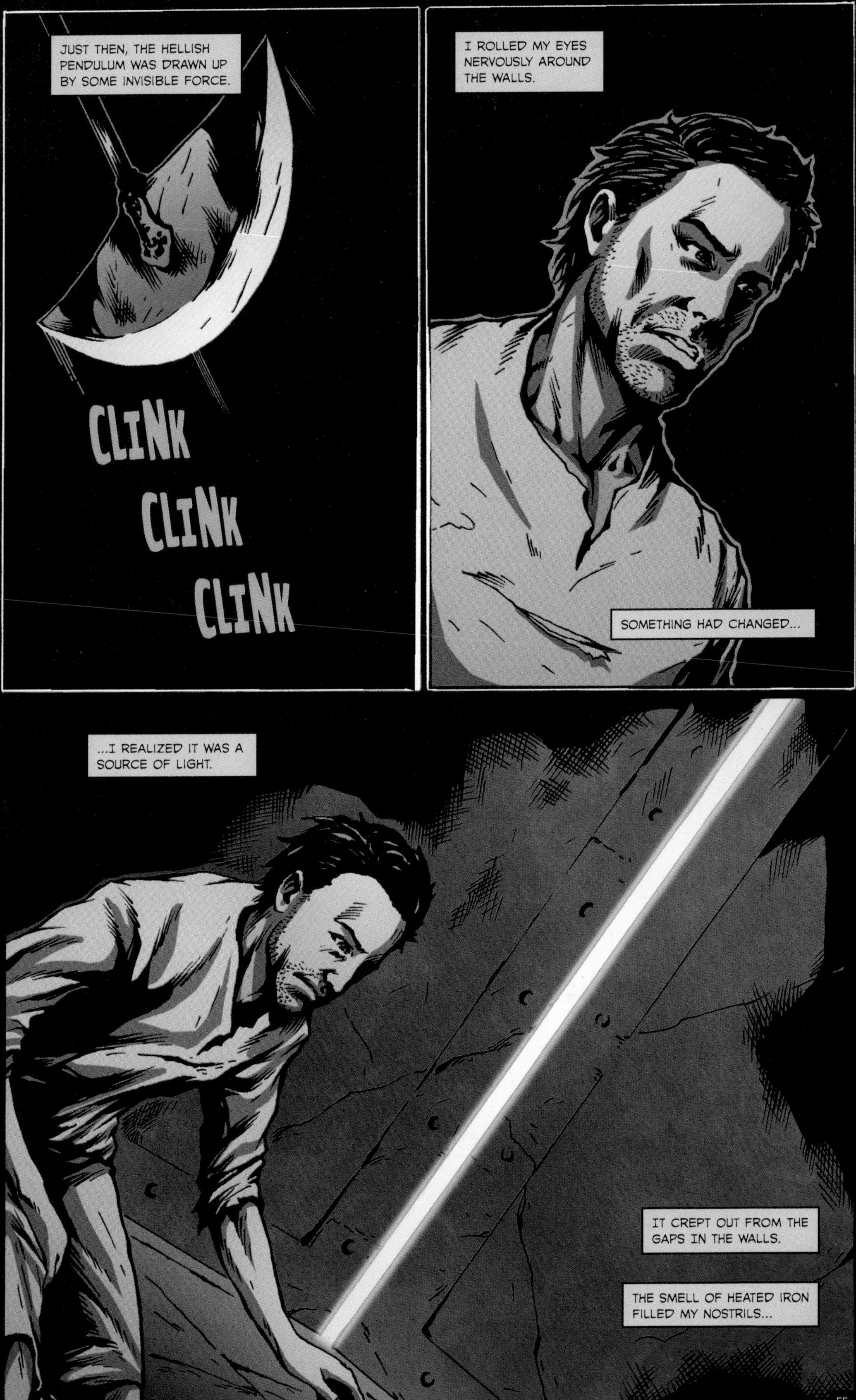
JUST THEN, THE HELLISH PENDULUM WAS DRAWN UP BY SOME INVISIBLE FORCE.
CLINK
CLINK
CLINK
I ROLLED MY EYES NERVOUSLY AROUND THE WALLS.
SOMETHING HAD CHANGED...
...I REALIZED IT WAS A SOURCE OF LIGHT.
IT CREPT OUT FROM THE GAPS IN THE WALLS.
THE SMELL OF HEATED IRON FILLED MY NOSTRILS...

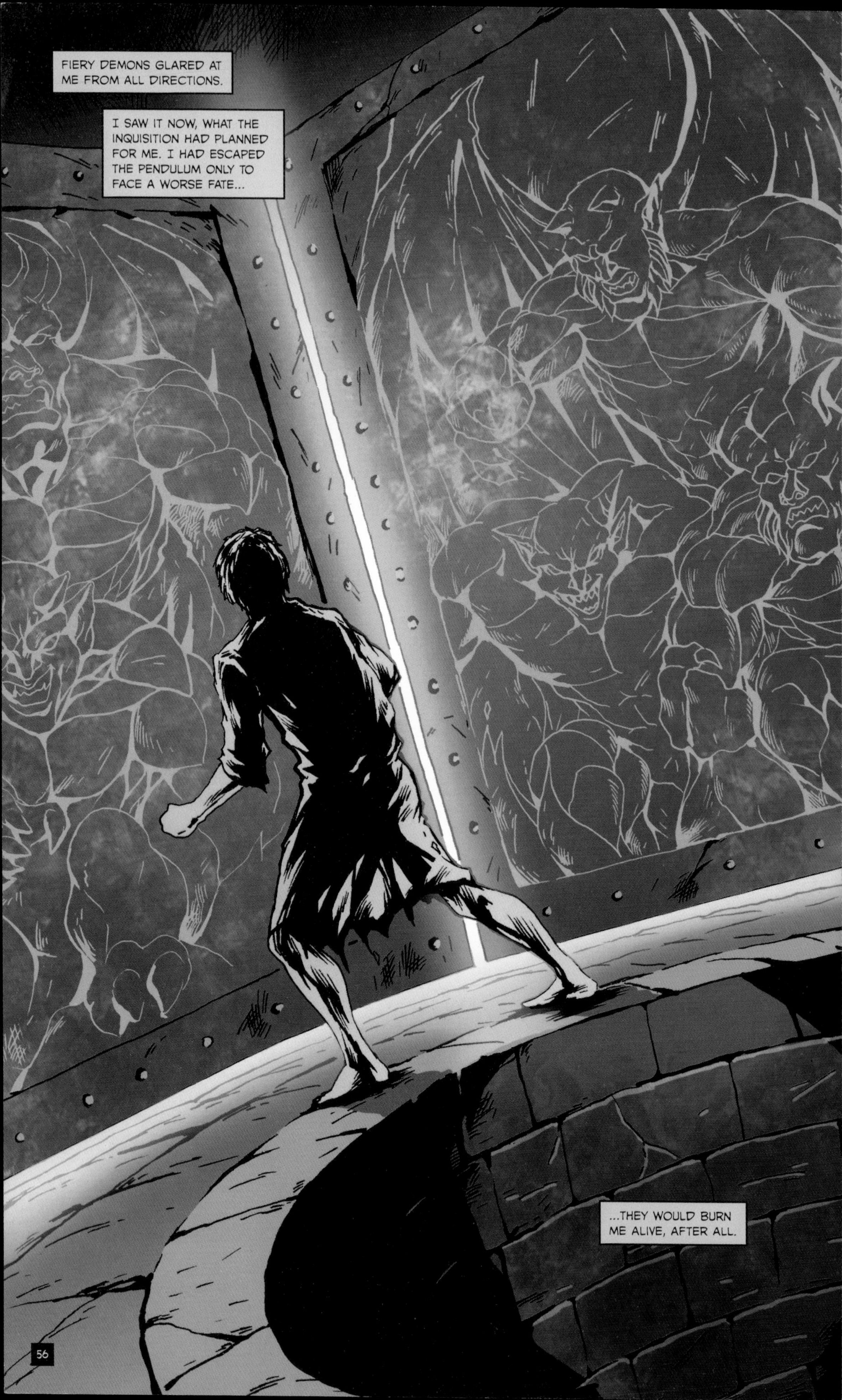

FIERY DEMONS GLARED AT ME FROM ALL DIRECTIONS.
I SAW IT NOW, WHAT THE INQUISITION HAD PLANNED FOR ME. I HAD ESCAPED THE PENDULUM ONLY TO FACE A WORSE FATE...
...THEY WOULD BURN ME ALIVE, AFTER ALL.

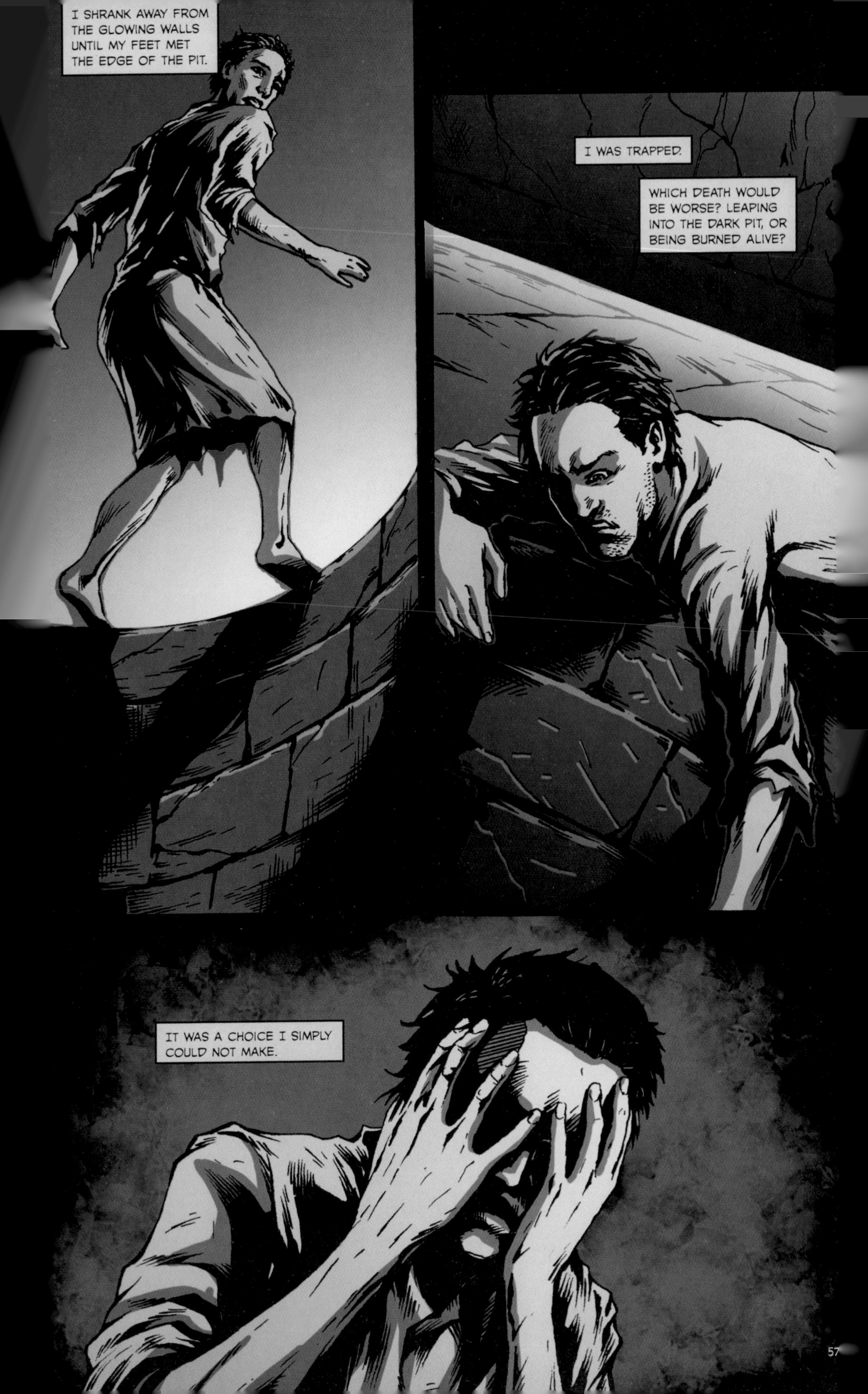
I SHRANK AWAY FROM THE GLOWING WALLS UNTIL MY FEET MET THE EDGE OF THE PIT.
I WAS TRAPPED.
WHICH DEATH WOULD BE WORSE? LEAPING INTO THE DARK PIT, OR BEING BURNED ALIVE?
IT WAS A CHOICE I SIMPLY COULD NOT MAKE.

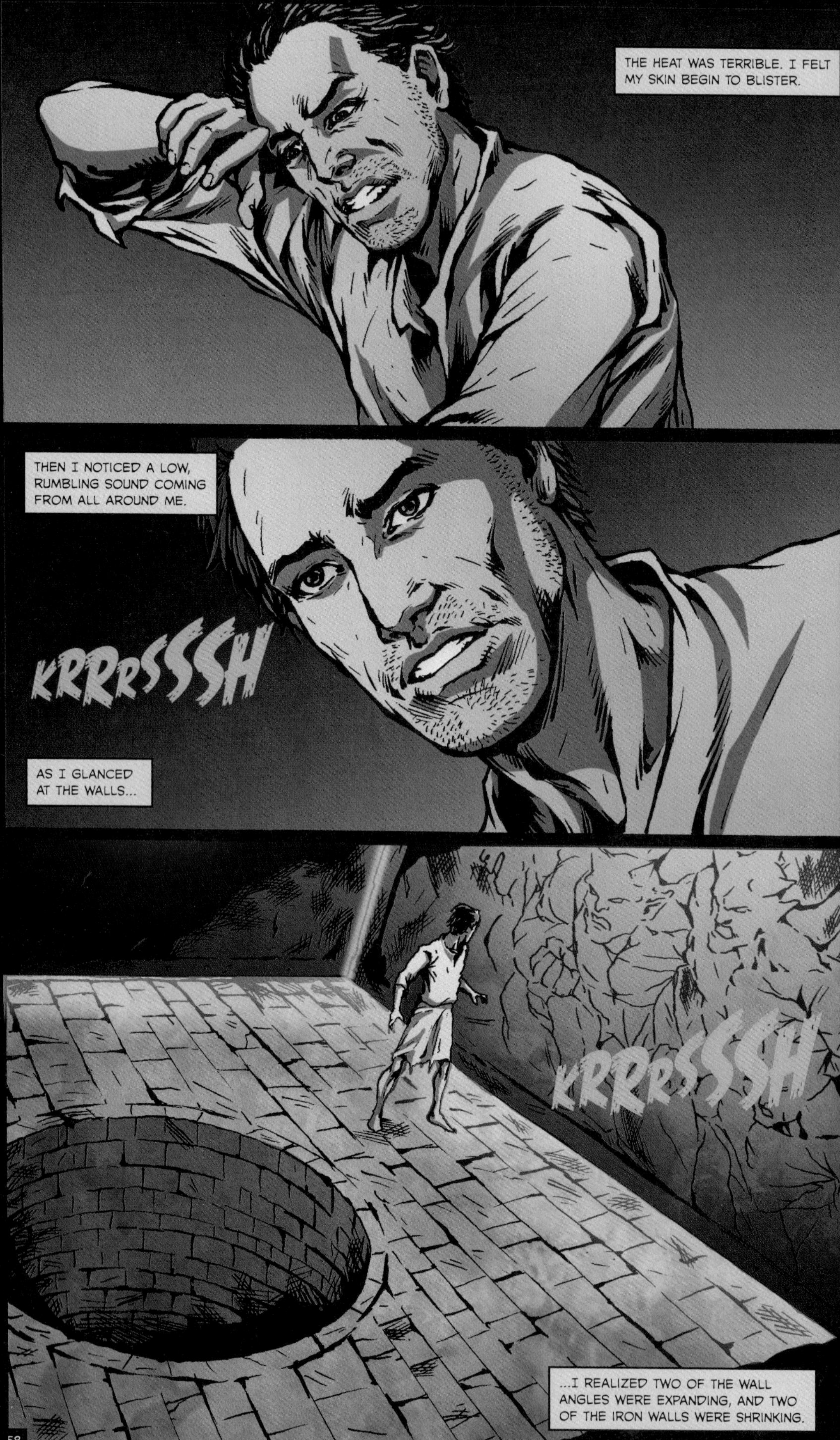
THE HEAT WAS TERRIBLE. I FELT MY SKIN BEGIN TO BLISTER.
THEN I NOTICED A LOW, RUMBLING SOUND COMING FROM ALL AROUND ME.
KRRRSSSH
AS I GLANCED AT THE WALLS...
KRRRSSSH
...I REALIZED TWO OF THE WALL ANGLES WERE EXPANDING, AND TWO OF THE IRON WALLS WERE SHRINKING.

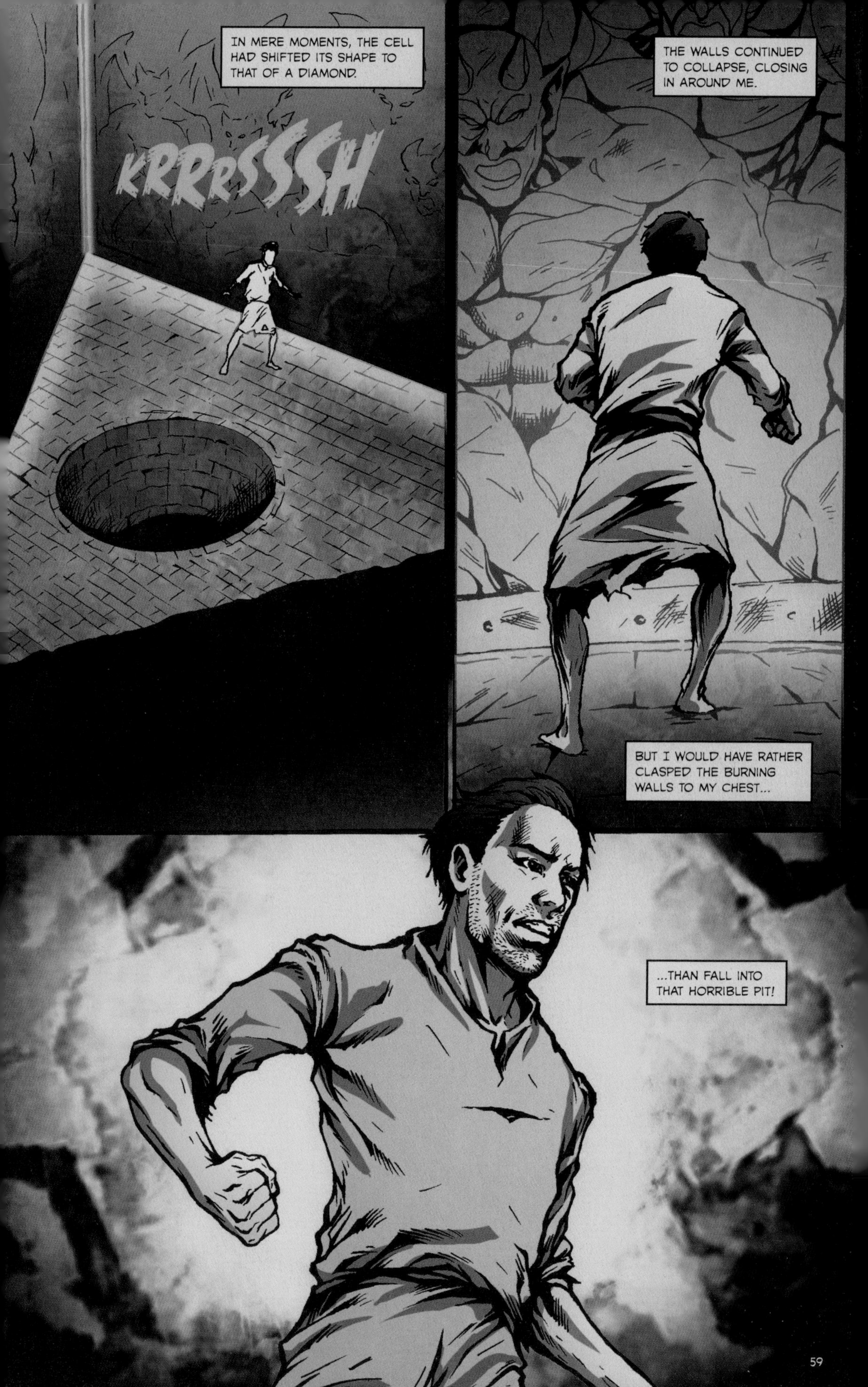
IN MERE MOMENTS, THE CELL HAD SHIFTED ITS SHAPE TO THAT OF A DIAMOND.
KRRRSSSH
THE WALLS CONTINUED TO COLLAPSE, CLOSING IN AROUND ME.
BUT I WOULD HAVE RATHER CLASPED THE BURNING WALLS TO MY CHEST...
...THAN FALL INTO THAT HORRIBLE PIT!

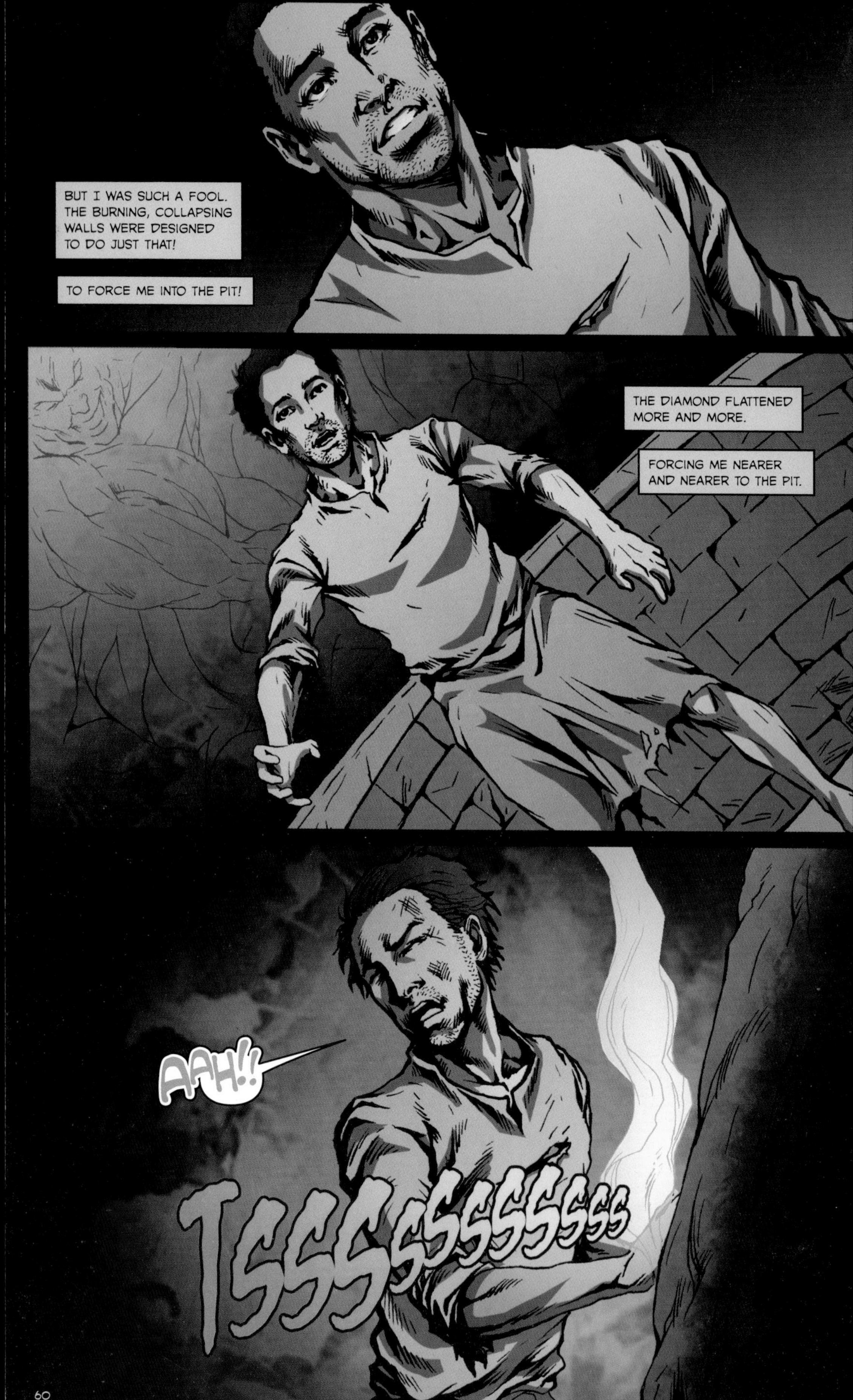
BUT I WAS SUCH A FOOL. THE BURNING, COLLAPSING WALLS WERE DESIGNED TO DO JUST THAT!
TO FORCE ME INTO THE PIT!
THE DIAMOND FLATTENED MORE AND MORE.
FORCING ME NEARER AND NEARER TO THE PIT.
AAH!!
TSSSSSSSSSSSS

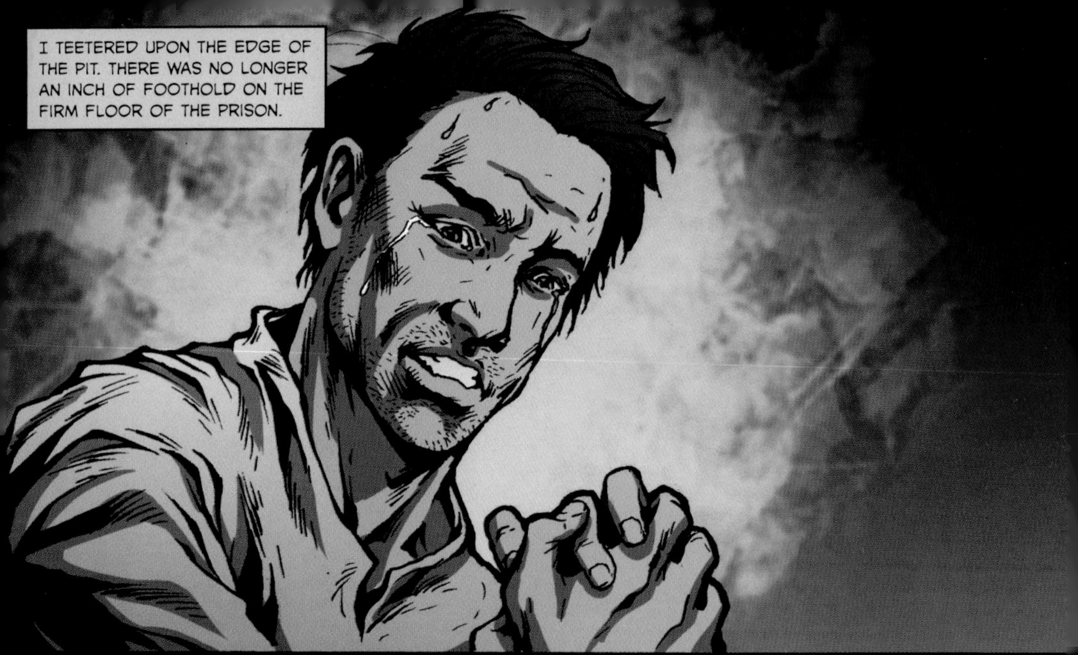
I TEETERED UPON THE EDGE OF THE PIT. THERE WAS NO LONGER AN INCH OF FOOTHOLD ON THE FIRM FLOOR OF THE PRISON.

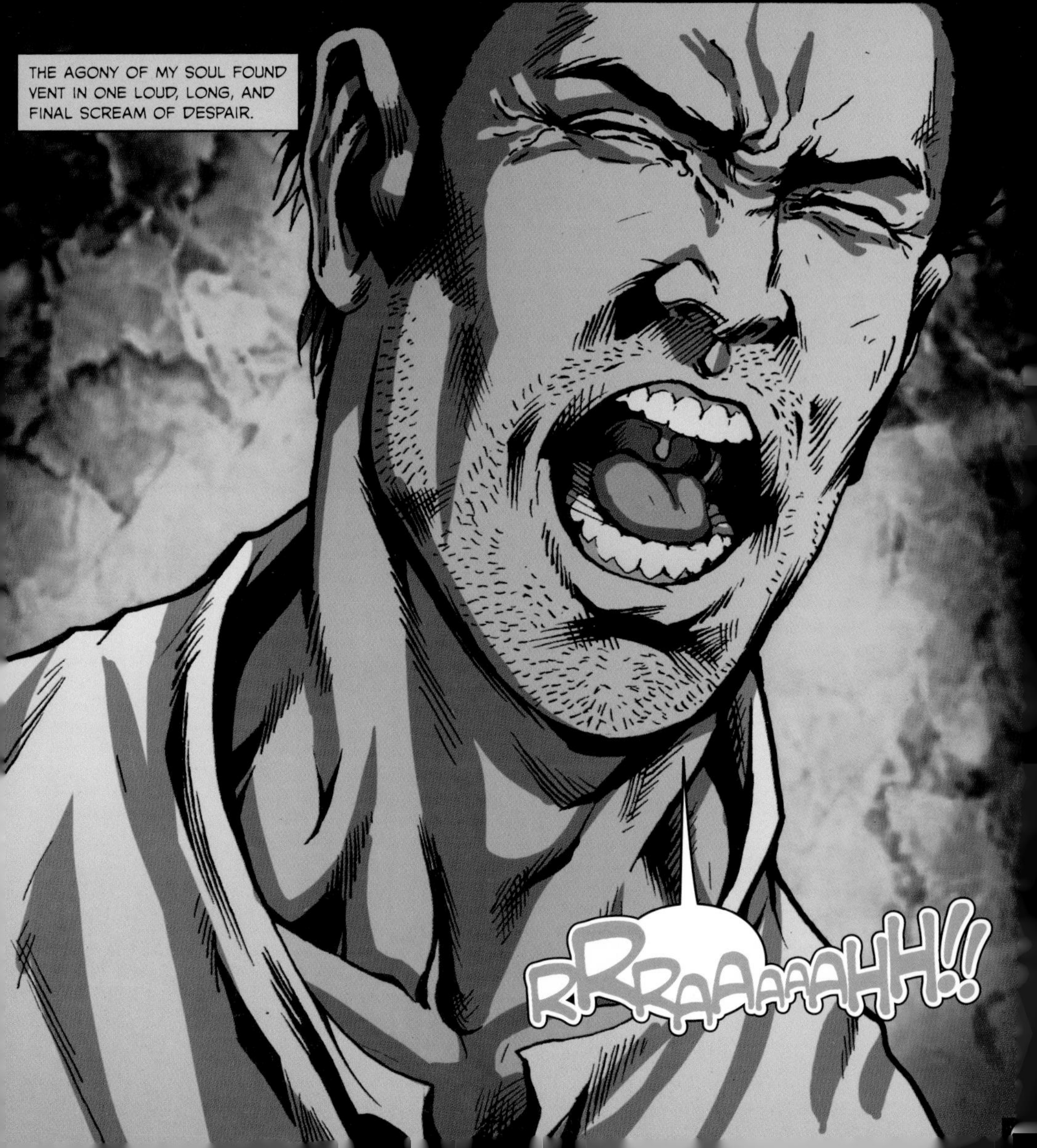
THE AGONY OF MY SOUL FOUND VENT IN ONE LOUD, LONG, AND FINAL SCREAM OF DESPAIR.
RRRAAAAAAHH!!

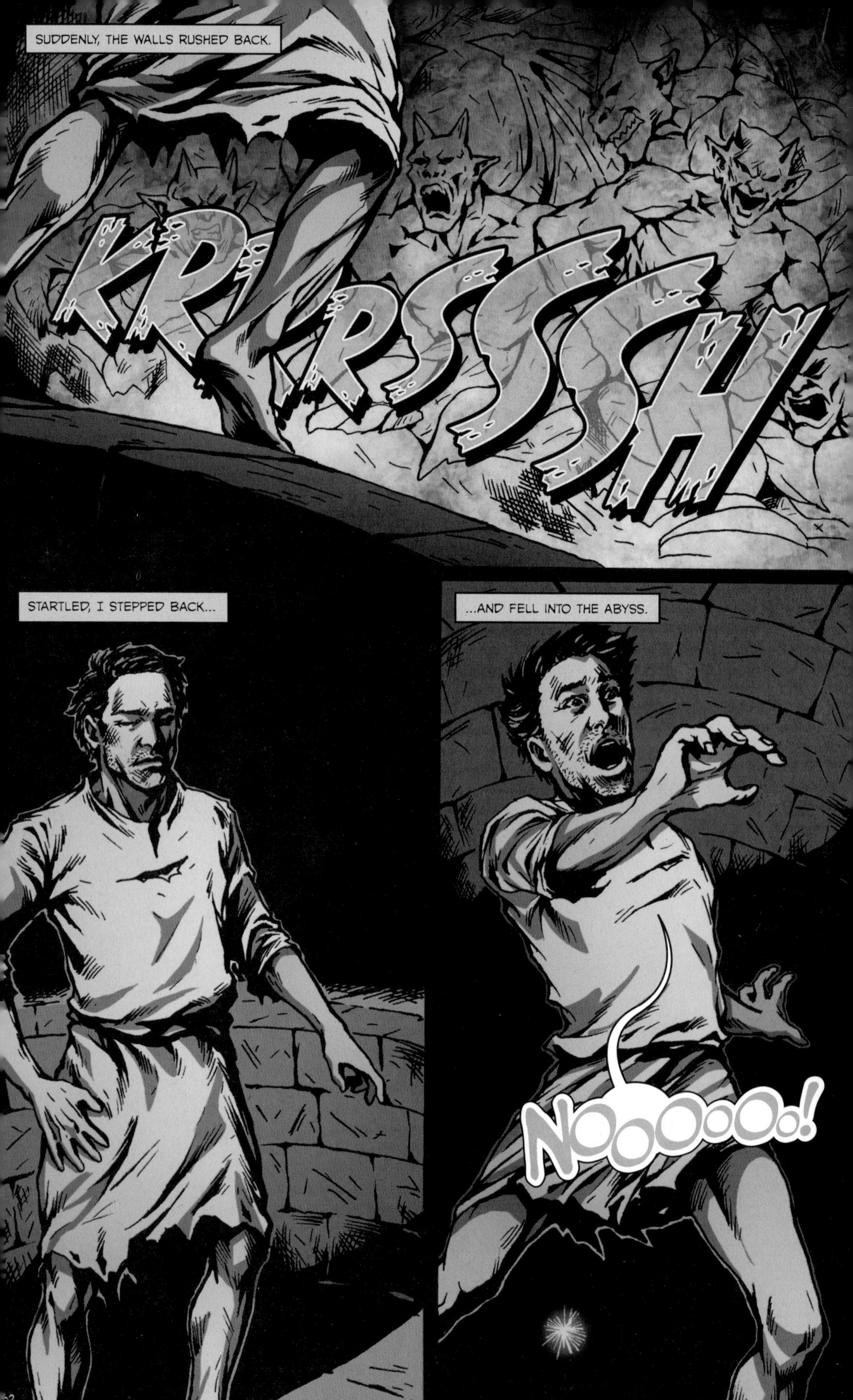
SUDDENLY, THE WALLS RUSHED BACK.
KRRSSSH
STARTLED, I STEPPED BACK...
...AND FELL INTO THE ABYSS.
NOOOOOO!

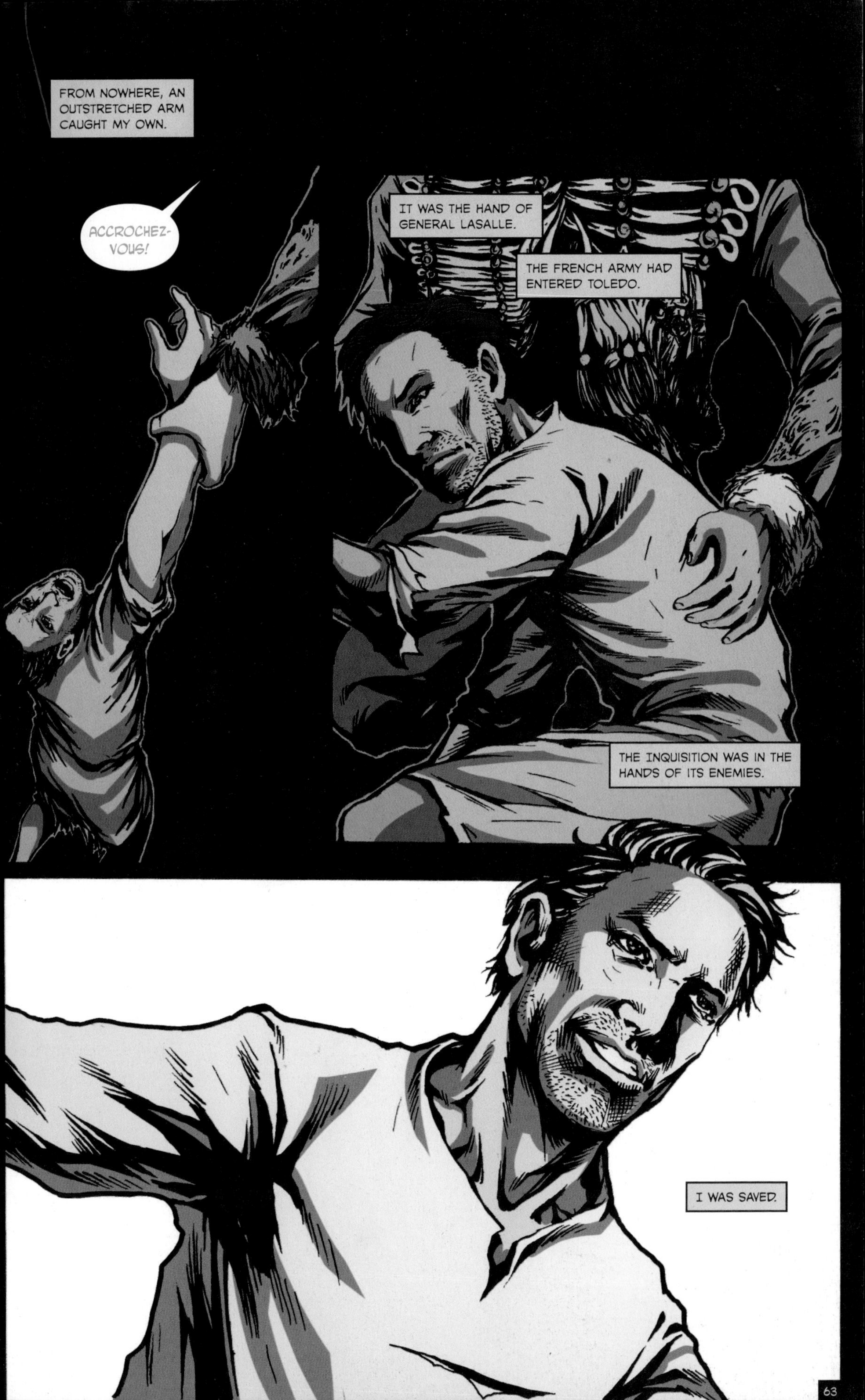
FROM NOWHERE, AN OUTSTRETCHED ARM CAUGHT MY OWN.
ACCROCHEZ-VOUS!
IT WAS THE HAND OF GENERAL LASALLE.
THE FRENCH ARMY HAD ENTERED TOLEDO.
THE INQUISITION WAS IN THE HANDS OF ITS ENEMIES.
I WAS SAVED.

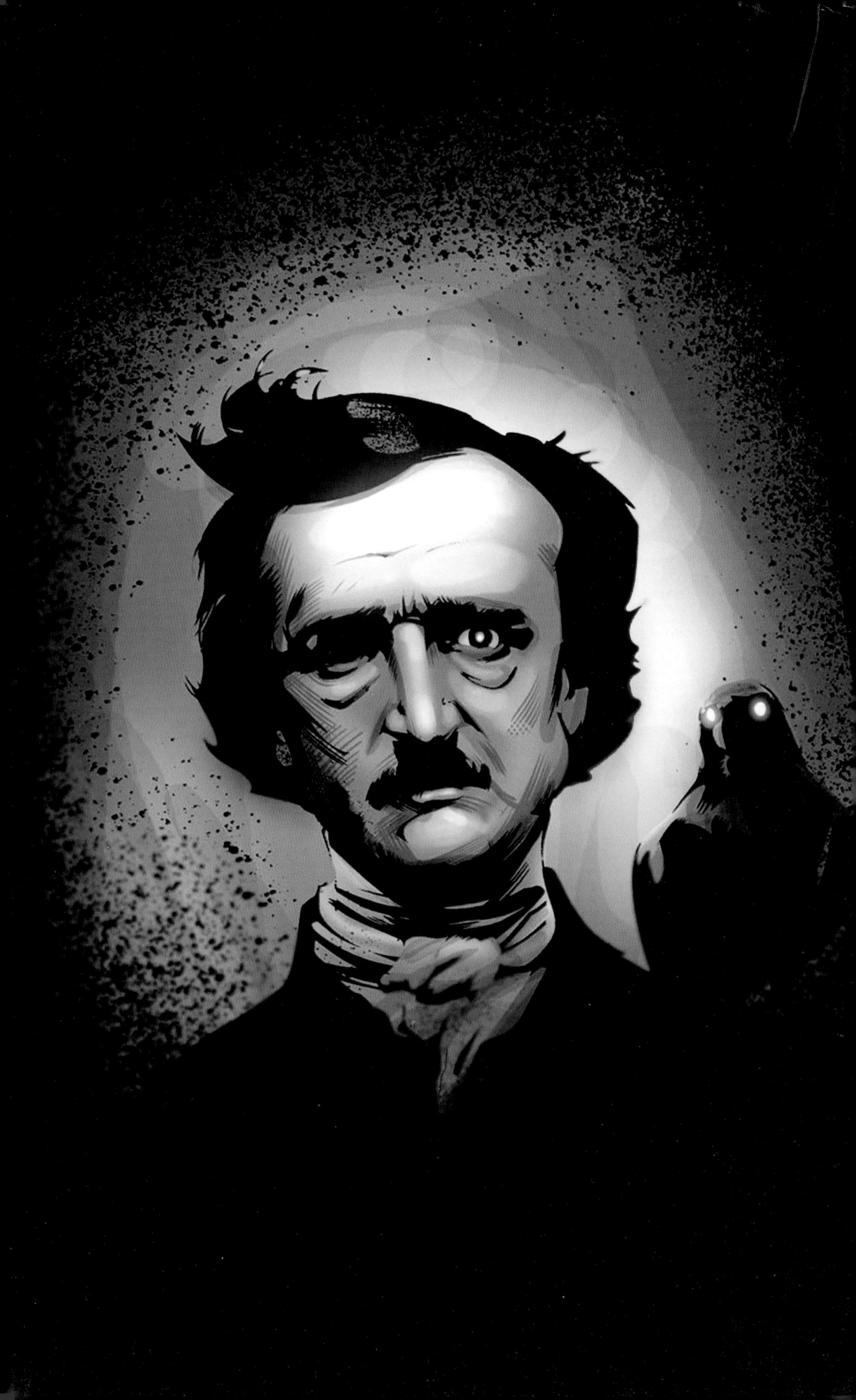

Over the course of his life, Edgar Allan Poe submitted many stories and poems to a number of publications. All of them were either rejected, or he received little to no compensation for them. His most popular work, "The Raven", quite nearly made him a household name—but only earned him nine dollars.

Poe was unable to hold a single job for very long, jumping from position to position for most of his life. He had very few friends, was in constant financial trouble, and struggled with alcoholism throughout his adult years. Edgar's family rarely helped him during these difficult times. In fact, when Edgar's father died in 1834, he did not even mention Edgar in his will.

Though largely unappreciated in his own lifetime, Edgar Allan Poe is now recognized as one of the most important writers of American literature.

THE RETELLING AUTHOR

SEAN TULIEN is a children's book editor living and working in Minnesota. In his spare time, he likes to read, eat sushi, ride his mountain bike, listen to loud music, watch unsettling movies, and write books like this one.

THE ILLUSTRATOR

J.C. FABUL grew up in Palawan, Philippines, and now lives in Manila. He studied Fine Arts in college, earning a degree in Painting. Illustrating comics is a big part of his life, but he also does digital illustration, portraiture, art commissions, and sketch cards.

GLOSSARY

ABYSS (uh-BISS)--a very deep hole that seems to have no bottom

AGONY (AG-uh-nee)--great pain or suffering

CIRCUIT (SUR-kit)--a journey beginning and ending in the same spot

DECAYING (di-KAY-ing)--the rotting or breaking down of plant or animal matter by natural causes

DESPAIR (di-SPAIR)--to lose hope completely

DREADFUL (DRED-fuhl)--very frightening, awful, or bad

ETERNAL (i-TUR-nuhl)--lasting forever

HIDEOUS (HID-ee-uhss)--ugly or horrible

INQUISITION (in-kwuh-ZISH-uhn)--an official investigation of a political or religious nature that is known for violating individual rights, prejudice on the part of the judges, and cruel punishments

LOCUTION (loh-KYOO-shuhn)--speech or verbal expression

REJOICED (ri-JOISSD)--happily celebrated

RELIEF (ri-LEEF)--a feeling of freedom from pain or worry

WRITHE (RITHE)--to twist and turn, as if in pain

The Inquisition intended to make the Narrator's imprisonment as unpleasant as possible. Look through this book and find several examples of ways they made the Narrator suffer.

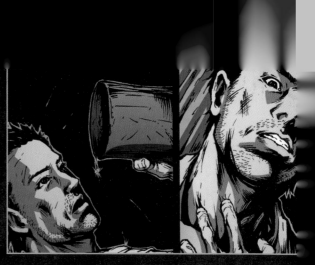

2. The Narrator goes through a series of different emotions on pages 46–47. For each panel, describe the emotion you think the Narrator is feeling based on the captions, color, and the illustrations.

3. Why do you think Poe included a painting of Time, or Father Time, on the ceiling of the dungeon? [Page 38.]

4. The Narrator has a few nightmares or hallucinations in this book. Explain how the nightmares or hallucinations are related to his experiences.

5. Identify several panels in this book where fear twisted the Narrator's memories, thoughts, or perspective.

6. The final panel in this book [page 63] shows the Narrator set against a white background. How does it differ from the rest of the book? Why do you think the panel is illustrated in this way?

INTRODUCING ANOTHER POE GRAPHIC NOVEL...

THE FALL OF THE HOUSE OF USHER

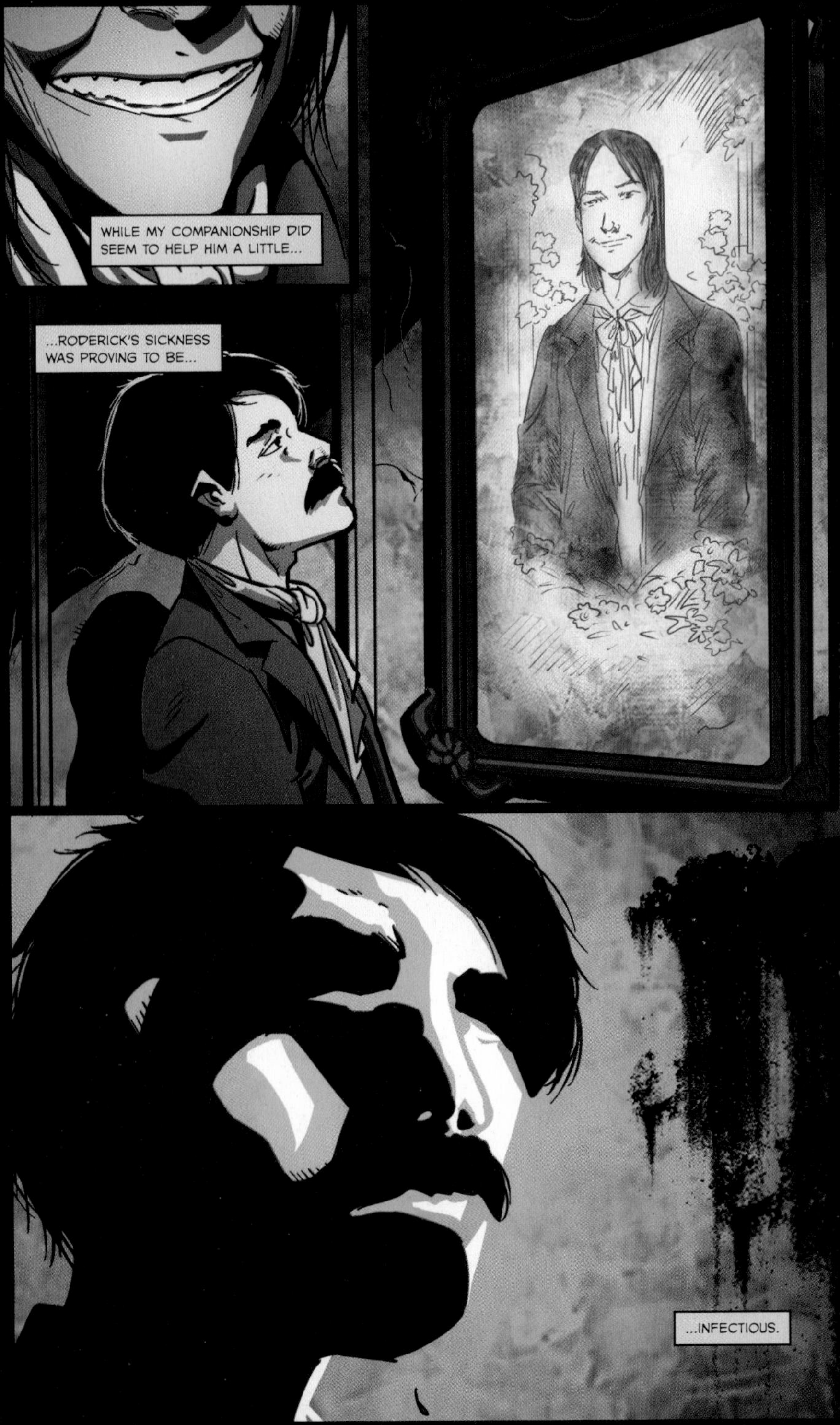
WHILE MY COMPANIONSHIP DID SEEM TO HELP HIM A LITTLE...
...RODERICK'S SICKNESS WAS PROVING TO BE...
...INFECTIOUS.